Final Lock

Books by Christine Marshall
With illustrations by Steve Marshall

Becoming Cinder
White As Snow
Forever Sleeping
Promised Beauty
Final Lock
Little Flower

RISE of the GIANTS
BATTLE of the GIANTS
LAST of the GIANTS

The Last Mapmaker
A Series of Intentional Disasters
Volume 1, Volume 2, Volume 3

NOBLESTONE and the Lost Dwarves
NOBLESTONE and the Secret Forge

Illustrated Guides:
Dragons and Flying Creatures
Folk Creatures
Unexpected Creatures
Insects and Mechanical Things

Final Lock

A Retelling

Christine Marshall

This book is dedicated to
Hannah and her long, blonde
locks at five years old. Your
hair is an inspiration to us all.

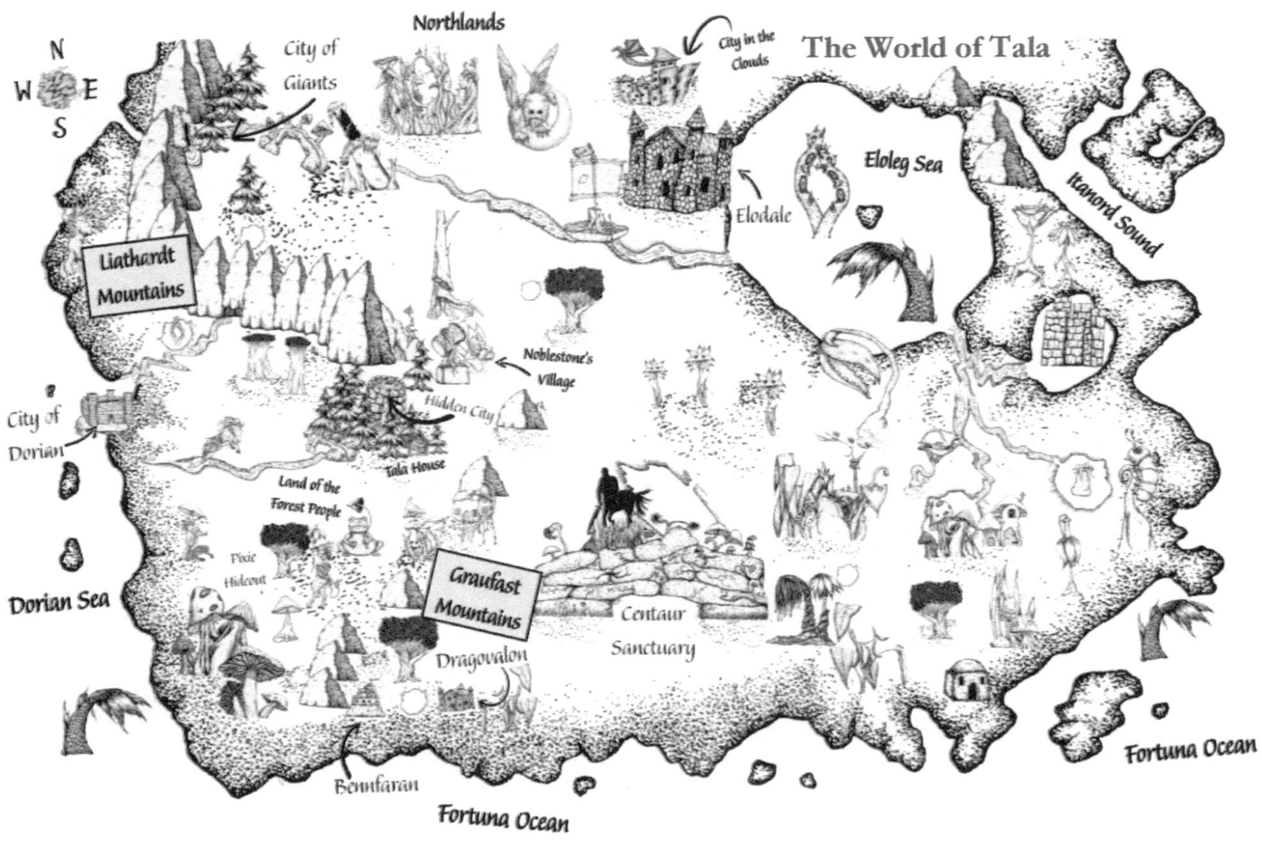

Learn more about **Tala** at the back of the book!

Chapter 1

Lock-picking requires specific knowledge about the type of lock that a smith- or thief- decides to manipulate.

Some locks can be cracked with the right amount of finesse.

Others require skill.

Some can only be broken with a little bit of pixie magic.

They all require tools. A wide variety of tools.

Zinnie brushed her slender fingers over the carefully organized selection of tools lined up like soldiers ready for battle. A series of finger-length rods with smooth handles on one end and different tips on the other. Keys, picks, hooks, points, wavy, straight, crimped. All hand made by Zinnie herself.

Her skill with these tools rivaled even the best kinds of pixie magic.

Some experts kept their tools on an iron ring, like keys. She preferred a felt pouch, with a pocket for each tool, that could be rolled up and tucked away out of sight.

Much quieter.

Much more secure.

Much easier to hide.

Which tools were right for this job? Her fingers settled on a stylus with a hook end, kind of like a fancy embroidery hook.

Embroidery. A useless pastime for most young women. Not so useless for Zinnie.

She pinched the handle between two nimble fingers with delicate precision.

Her second tool choice featured a thick, flat head, which she held firmly in her other hand.

"These should do the trick." She kept her voice low.

She maneuvered the pair of tools into the lock and kept her eyes focused on her work in the near-darkness.

Her ears, however, tuned to her surroundings. She automatically disregarded the clop of minotaur hooves on cobblestone streets and the clatter of uneven wheels and poorly constructed carts of the early morning delivery services.

The steady rhythm of expensive brownie-made shoes clicking against the stones piqued her interest, but the sound faded as quickly as it had arrived. She hadn't been spotted.

Not surprising. Between the dark cloak covering her tangle of bright blonde braids and unladylike black trousers, plus the early pre-dawn light, she was well hidden in the shadows.

When her fingers felt the click of the release inside the lock, Zinnie smoothly- and silently- pulled the lock open and set it carefully on the sill of the window. She returned her tools to their homes and stashed the rolled-up pouch underneath her front-laced bodice layered over her dark cotton blouse.

The window did not make a sound or resist in the slightest

as she pushed it inward at a moss-sloth's pace. In one fluid movement, she slipped over the sill and into the black room. A quick glance proved she was alone, and she turned to press the window closed again.

Something rustled outside the open door that led to the lobby of the building.

Zinnie froze. She forced her breathing to remain calm and her heart to remain steady. No one knew she was there. She blended with the shadows.

She turned her head just the slightest to peek over her shoulder. The cloak blocked her view of the room.

She remained still.

No one sounded an alarm or cried out. No flickering candlelight bounced off the walls or cast shadows into the room.

She took silent steps across the room, around the plush armchairs, and toward the door. She pressed herself against the wall and peered around the opening.

Something moved across the lobby. It darted between the shadows. Close to the ground.

Either a large rat or a small cat. She let out a tiny sigh of relief. Rats and cats were the least of her concerns.

She slipped down the hall toward another door that stood firmly closed.

"I hope my information was accurate," she whispered.

She removed a hair pin from her braids and slid it into the hole in the handle of the door. This lock only took finesse. Anyone could crack it. She couldn't believe that the proprietor even thought it to be secure.

A click from inside the lock tingled the hairs in her ears. She replaced the hair pin and entered the room.

"Jackpot."

Her eyes, well-adjusted to the darkness like a dwarf in an underground home, mapped the windowless room. The complex blend of aromas stung her nose. She held back a sneeze.

Shelves lined with decorated jars, unique-shaped vials, dipped candles, blocks of charcoal soaps, and strips of linen cloth rolled into bandages, stretched floor to ceiling on one side.

The second wall held hooks with drying bundles of herbs, leaves, and flowers; cubbies full of roots, wood chips, and barks; baskets of blossoms and nuts; and containers for animal parts and fluids. She even spotted a small glass globe filled with writhing leeches. She shivered.

Books in disarray filled the shelves on the final wall. Papers stuck out from journals; thick volumes of loose-leaf notes stacked precariously on top of one another; and boxes for reference cards heaped in a haphazard fashion.

A large butcher block style table filled the center of the room. It held scales, cooking tools, root cutters, and other equipment used to measure, prepare, and package the various liniments, potions, and pills that the apothecary produced.

She pulled her cross-body satchel from behind her back and held it open with one hand. She methodically circled the room and placed the required items into her bag, careful to be silent as a domestic flower troll the entire time.

The proprietor would be asleep on the second floor, alone. His wife and children away visiting relatives in another city. His apprentice was ill, along with a good portion of the citizens of the city.

The man was overworked and tired from this week's business, especially with the sweating sickness going around the city as of late.

He slept as if he were a neutralized stone golem.

Just the same, Zinnie remained silent in her task. She buckled her bag closed and shifted it behind her again.

A small bag of sea pearls placed in the center of the table

helped ease her guilty conscience. No one needed to know that the very person who stole the supplies had left them behind.

She made sure the lock on the door handle was engaged before the door clicked into place as she snuck from the room.

Another rustle tickled her ears. A scurry of tiny claws on the wood floor. Something brushed against her exposed ankle. A shadow skimmed along the floorboards.

Zinnie sucked in a sharp breath and recoiled. Her elbow banged against the wall. The contents of the shelves on the other side rattled.

She leapt away from the wall, afraid of hitting it again.

Her foot stepped on something soft.

A yowl pierced the air. Claws tore into her ankle.

She yiped from the pain and slapped her hand over her mouth.

Zinnie froze. Her eyes darted at the ceiling.

Would the man awake?

She waited a breath, and looked at the creature that had clawed at her ankle after she had accidentally stepped on one of its leathery wings.

The orange, winged feline with a stinger on its hard tail glared at her through the darkness with its glowing green eyes. It curled the barbed tail up and over its body, turned away from Zinnie, and bounded back the way it had come.

She counted to three. So far, so good.

She rushed down the hall back to the door of the study she had entered the shop through.

A loud "Oof" came from upstairs followed by the sound of the cat being dropped onto the floor.

Zinnie snuck back into the study and hid behind the door as it stood ajar. Should she close it? Would the man know he had left it open the previous night and notice it out of place?

She pressed herself against the wall and willed herself to remain perfectly still.

The man thumped down the stairs like he had consumed too much ale, but she knew it was just because of his extreme fatigue.

That's why she had him as her mark. It was the perfect storm to steal from him. He would be asleep and not notice a thing. In his haze the following morning, he would probably just think he had run out of or misplaced the items she had procured.

Everything had gone perfectly.

Until that miniature manticore startled her. She stepped on its wing.

And now the man tromped down the stairs. To look around? Or perhaps maybe just for a midnight snack? Maybe he was sleepwalking!

Whatever the reason, she could not risk being caught.

He shuffled down the hall, past her open door, and toward the back of the building.

What if he checked on his supply? What if he suspected something?

She darted to the window, opened it quickly, but quietly, and threw her legs over the sill. The jars in her bag clinked against one another and she scolded herself.

"Slow down, Zinnie."

She extended her legs, dropped to the ground, and ducked below the window.

Footsteps echoed inside the room. Shadows announced his approach. The man had lit a candle. Zinnie could no longer rely on blending into the shadows if he caught her.

"What the…" He stopped at the open window.

Zinnie clenched her jaw. She squeezed her eyes shut and huddled beneath her cloak.

The man fumbled with the lock Zinnie had left on the windowsill. He mumbled under his breath in a gravelly voice about flower trolls and brownies poking their noses where they did not belong. He leaned out the window to have a look around outside.

This was it. She would be caught. Thrown into the dungeon to never see the light of day again.

Sweat beaded on her forehead. She sunk deeper into her cloak. Into the shadows that the impending sunrise would soon brighten. The murmurs of the man just above her head held Zinnie captive.

Chapter 2

"Gyb, you nuisance of a cat!" The apothecary let out an exasperated sigh when the orange manticore jumped onto the windowsill. Its paws padded back and forth across the frame. The leathery wings creaked as they folded and unfolded.

The man's nightclothes rustled when he pushed the cat off the sill. Its paws thumped just opposite Zinnie on the inside of the structure.

A clang of metal on wood immediately followed the sound of the manticore's return to the floor.

Zinnie couldn't believe her luck! The lock had been knocked to the floor. The man would bend over to pick it up. This was her chance to slip away.

She didn't hesitate. She waited one beat for the sleepy man to figure out what he must do. She crouch-walked along the wall of the building and slipped around the corner.

She didn't dare look back.

Her feet beat a steady rhythm on the cobblestones as she wove her way through the City of Dorian to return home.

The City of Dorian had been built in an irregular manner. Markets, shops, craftsmen, and pubs mingled with homes, meeting halls, and stables with no apparent pattern. Anyone from outside the city found it impossible to locate anything without the help of someone familiar with the place.

Perhaps that was the plan all along. It allowed the residents of the city to "help" visitors. For a cost. *Everything* in Dorian cost someone something.

Zinnie passed the market carts that roamed the streets. The aroma of fresh baked bread mingled with animal droppings from the pack-animals that moved people and merchandise about. Mobile-farmer's-markets of fruits and vegetables, honey, skins and furs, and more, tried to lure customers away from the book makers, clothing vendors, and flower shops.

Each citizen of Dorian played a zero-sum game. If someone spent their hard-earned coins at one shop, they didn't have coins to spend at another. The competition was fierce. The proprietors ruthless.

The stench of burnt meat from a food vendor caused Zinnie's nose to wrinkle. She dodged that street and turned down another.

The further toward her destination she traveled, the busier and louder the city became. Morning had brought all the people and creatures out of their homes and the business of profit had begun in earnest. Her ears were assaulted by all the sounds of a busy city on a busy morning at the end of spring.

The sweating sickness had made its way through most of the residents over the past several months, and many were just starting to feel better. Which meant they had to make up for their lost days of money-making.

Fortunately, neither Zinnie nor her mistress had become very ill due to the herbs that were brewed into their tea every morning. And *maybe* something more. She had been instructed quite clearly to keep that information to herself.

"Hello, Lady!" One of the marketers waved from his place behind his mobile stand of counterfeit dwarf-crafted items. His smile lit up his face.

She swung her hand over her head and returned his smile. When she had discovered that his items were fake, he thought for sure she would turn him over to the authorities or share the information with her mistress. But Zinnie had promised to keep his secret, and she had been true to her word. The man had been so relieved he reminded her to come to him anytime she might need a tool or weapon and she would have it, free of charge. She settled for a cheerful greeting when they crossed paths.

The businesspeople may not appreciate *each other*, but they each appreciated the girl who carried valuable information and useful skills. And who knew how to keep secrets.

One never knew when they would need to hire a pickpocket, have a secret message to send, or dabble in a little bit of minor blackmail. Zinnie knew the reason they treated her well, but she didn't mind. She was an asset, nothing more. Besides, weren't they all just trying to survive, the same as herself? Her mistress constantly reminded her that all of her connections made her invaluable to her mistress, otherwise she would be a sad, lonely girl like so many others.

"Flower for the flower girl?" The middle-aged florist held a lavender stained carnation toward Zinnie.

"Thank you, Camilia." Zinnie nodded her head and buried her nose in the blossom. Normally carnations didn't have much of a scent, but Camilia watered hers with lavender scented water. Zinnie's shoulders relaxed at the soothing smell.

"If you hear any rumors of those flower trolls popping up, make sure you remind the people that they don't come from my crop, will you?" Camilia spoke in a conspiratorial tone with Zinnie.

The truth was flower trolls were hard to control. Camilia had no way of preventing them from infiltrating the homes of her patrons any better than any other florist did.

"Always." She shook the woman's dirt-smudged hand and thanked her again for the blossom as she tucked it above her ear.

"How about a sweet for my sweet?" A graying man wearing a dingy apron around his neck handed Zinnie a warm paper-wrapped pastry as she walked by.

"Mmmm! You know me too well, Baxter! I owe you for this one!"

Baxter waved away her comment. "No, it's free, as always." He winked his wrinkly eye and grinned a lopsided smile at her.

"You're too kind."

As usual, she shared half of the pastry with a hungry looking child and munched on her own half as she walked.

When the pastry had vanished and the paper discarded, Zinnie licked the sticky sugar from her fingers.

She skirted around the alley that led to her destination, opting for the slightly longer but definitely safer route. Unkind ogres tended to hang out in places like that.

Not that she couldn't defend herself if she needed to. She

had been trained in the finer arts that other young women learn. But her benefactor had also insisted she learn skills that some would consider less-savory for a young girl. Good thing she had learned them all in secret.

Now, as a seventeen-year-old almost-woman, she could blend in with the high society- provided she had the appropriate clothing and adornments available. Which she didn't... most of the time. She had made friends with those who could provide her with what she needed, so it never became a problem when the need arose.

She could also hold her own against any number of threats, including grumpy ogres, but why put herself in harm's way? She would only be a few minutes late by taking the longer route. Her mistress wouldn't be *that* upset. Probably.

The clanking of the bottles in her bag urged her feet to move faster, but not so fast that she would risk breaking them.

Zinnie's keen eyes took in her surroundings like a jewelry appraiser. Another trick she had learned in her less-than-ideal upbringing.

A flock of butterfly dragons scarfed on the gory remains of some animal. A kangaroo rat, or something like it. They were like scaly vultures that breathed fire on the meat before they consumed it.

She turned the last corner around the lopsided building that tilted precariously to one side. Only a few doors to go.

The building angled over the street, supported by added beams and scaffolding. It was a miracle the building didn't collapse into a heap of rubble.

Zinnie hesitated in front of the patched up wooden door with a painted-over window. The other windows along the back of the building were so grimy that they were impossible to see through anymore.

She took a deep breath before entering the only home she had ever known. And she immediately regretted it. Her nose filled with the musty smell of this part of the city. No sweet breads or scented candles or spiced apothecaries here to sweeten the air.

Some day, she told herself, she would escape this place and live far away from anyone. On her own. No one telling her what to do or where to go or when to be home. No terrible smells or loud noises or anything. Just herself and the world.

But for now, she must put on a contented smile and enter the building. Deep down she knew that the idea of ever really being able to leave was just a fantasy. Nothing more.

The door creaked when she pushed it open. She entered a small kitchen, barely large enough for two people to stand or sit at the same time.

A kettle hung inside the fireplace. Steam billowed from the top and strong herbs stung Zinnie's nose. A blackened pot bubbled on the top of the stove. Zinnie lifted the lid. Porridge. As usual. Maybe there'd be some dry fruit to mask the stale flavor this time.

But her mistress was not there. She dropped the false smile from her face, sunk into one of the two wobbly chairs by the door, leaned her head against the wall, and closed her eyes. Her body relaxed and she rested for the few minutes of peace that she would have until her mistress realized she had returned.

Zinnie startled awake a few moments later. Her hood slipped from her head to reveal her long blonde hair woven in a tangle of braids down her back. The wispy parts by her face curled and one fine clump stuck to her dark lashes.

She blew the hair away with her lips and hoisted herself to her feet. Some of the blonde locks fell over her shoulder and stretched down her chest to her waist. She picked up the strand and held it out in front of her. It was getting a little too long. Time for a trim.

Chapter 3

Zinnie had her own room. Her own *tiny* room. Just large enough for her narrow bed, a dresser chest two drawers high, a short side table beside her bed the size of a dinner plate, and a set of pegs on the wall alongside the door. She crossed from the door to her bed in two steps. And with her shorter than average legs, that was saying something.

Zinnie hung her cloak on one of the pegs, pulled the satchel over her head, disentangled it from her hair, and tossed it on the bed. It clinked.

"The bottles!" She snatched it up and opened it to examine its contents.

"Whew. All safe and sound."

She sunk onto the bed and leaned toward her side table.

"Hello, my flying jewel." She cooed at the iridescent-feathered animal perched inside the rusty circular cage.

She received a billow of smoke in reply.

Zinnie sighed. "I know, Lela. I'm sorry you've been stuck in there all night. But I couldn't risk bringing you on this job. I had to be absolutely silent! And it was a good thing. The man had a pet manticore! A kitten-sized one, but still…"

Lela, Zinnie's pet hummingbird-dragon, cocked her head to one side. Her golden eyes peered at Zinnie.

"Don't look at me like that!" Zinnie reached for the latch on the cage. She opened the hatch and motioned for Lela to emerge.

The dragon, only the length of Zinnie's palm, did not hesitate. She stretched her feathery wings and swooped out of the opening. She circled the room once and perched herself on Zinnie's hand. Her long, feathery tail wrapped around her four clawed feet- something of a cross between lizard and bird feet, meant for perching or walking. Her sharp talons poked Zinnie's palm but did not pierce the skin.

She let out another huff of white smoke from her nostrils.

Zinnie stroked her soft feathers.

The feathers on Lela's head fluffed into a crown.

"I'll bring you with me all day today, alright? But first, I need a haircut, don't you think?"

Zinnie tossed her long blond hair over her shoulder and stood.

Lela took to the air again and flapped her delicate wings so fast that they turned into a blur above her body. She stayed right beside Zinnie.

Zinnie sometimes felt strange talking to Lela as if the dragon could understand her, but Lela was her only friend. She interpreted the animal's movements and expressions as a sort of language, even if it was just make-believe. Besides, who ever heard of anyone in Dorian being able to talk to animals? No one that she knew of, though there were people out there, somewhere, who could.

When she asked her mistress about them during her studies the reply had been harsh. "Do not make up strange tales. And keep your wild imagination to yourself or others might think you do not have a solid grasp on reality."

She had taken a mental note to keep her curiosity to herself and only focus on the things right in front of her.

In this case, that would be her cracked mirror.

A close inspection caused her to frown. She could practically hear her mistress's superior voice. "You really should take more care in your appearance."

She sighed.

"First things first, Lela."

She dipped her hands into the bowl of water that sat beside the mirror. She cupped them and lifted them from the bowl.

"You ready?" She waited for the dragon to swoop and land in her cupped hands.

The dragon fluttered her feathers and dipped her head. Water rivulets ran down her back along her feathers and down her legs. She shook her body to spray the water off the outside and flapped her wigs. A mist of water poofed from the fast-beating wings and she hovered once more.

Zinnie dribbled the remaining water from her hands into a smaller empty bowl beside the larger one.

She splashed water from the larger bowl onto her face.

Lela zipped away and returned with a small hand towel clasped in two of her clawed feet for Zinnie to dry her face.

"Thanks, Lela. I forgot. Again!" Zinnie laughed at herself.

How could she remember every little detail about the comings and goings of a stuffy old apothecary and his family but not remember to fetch a towel for when she washed her own face?

Lela screeched. A tiny sound that made Zinnie smile.

"I know. Too many things on my mind, right?"

Zinnie washed her hands and arms next, and dabbed water around the back of her neck and along into the top part of her bodice. She would clean herself better another time. This was all she had time for today.

"Time for the hair."

Lela swooped and cooed at Zinnie, circled her head, and fanned her with her wings.

Zinnie pulled the leather hair ties from her bunches of braids and used her fingers to comb out each one. When she finished, her hair reached past her knees and hung in loose curls. The side part and waves beside her face gave her a more mature look. She wished she could embrace that all of the time. But that wasn't what her mistress expected. Or rather, demanded.

Zinnie sighed. Again.

Lela perched on the top of the mirror and tipped her head. She blinked three times at Zinnie.

Zinnie felt like Lela did this to comfort her when she was distressed. She grinned at her tiny friend.

"The sooner I get this over with, the better," she announced.

She pulled the packet of tools from beneath her bodice and rested it on the top of her dresser beside her comb, hair clips, leather hair ties, and ribbons. She spread it open and removed the pair of simple scissors from the last pouch.

She gazed at her reflection. She turned her head side to side, the long waves swayed with the movement.

She tapped the closed scissors against her lips and met Lela's gaze.

"How short do you think I should go this time?" She gestured at her shoulder.

Lela lifted her nose and looked away.

"Shorter?" Zinnie held her hand flat beside her chin.

Lela fluffed her feathers and nodded once.

Zinnie raised her eyebrows. "Really? Why so short?"

Lela lowered her eyelids and stared at Zinnie, unblinking.

Zinnie laughed. "Alright, alright. Fine."

She opened her scissors and gripped a section of her hair with her other hand.

"Remember that time I had to cut it as short as a boy?" She cringed at the memory. "Mistress needed me to pose as one for that job.

Before the long locks could float to the floor in a heap, Zinnie pinched each one between her fingers and carefully stretched it across the top of the dresser.

"Then there was that time that I forgot to cut it when I was supposed to. Boy did I get in trouble for that!" Zinnie added another long section to the growing pile on the dresser.

"My favorite though is just below chin length. It keeps it off my face and is easy to style as needed. You know, an up do for something fancy, or loose curls for a younger look."

Zinnie turned her head side to side to examine her work. She corrected a few uneven strands and nodded.

"You were right. This is the perfect one for today."

Lela kept her wings folded and scampered down the mirror frame onto the surface of the dresser. She stood beside the pile of leather hair ties and picked one up with one clawed foot. She gave Zinnie an expectant look.

Zinnie returned the scissors to her case. She expertly wove the long strands into a thick braid, tying each end with one of the leather hair ties.

The dragon stretched her wings and swooped onto the floor just at the edge of Zinnie's bed.

Zinnie knelt beside her, the long braid in one hand. She pulled a case out from beneath her bed. The dragon fiddled with the lock with her long talons and gave Zinnie a satisfied look when the case popped open.

"Glad you are such a quick learner!" Zinnie stroked her friend along her back with one finger.

She carefully placed the braid inside the case, alongside at least two dozen other ones. Some as long as today's, others at varying lengths shorter than this one. She never could bring herself to discard the long pieces. Besides, the last thing she needed was for someone to notice the strands and start asking too many questions.

After the case was locked and returned under the bed, Zinnie stripped off her dark colored bodice and skirt and replaced them with brighter, fresher clothes. Muslin gauze wrapped tightly around her chest gave her a younger appearance. A lavender bodice and shin length matching skirt, with lace lined sleeves and matching waist tie, gave the impression of immaturity.

She tied purple ribbons into two half braids on either side of her head and spun around to assess her appearance.

"That should please Mistress. I look no more than thirteen in these clothes." She glanced at Lela.

The dragon let out a stream of fire. It was barely enough to light a match. Not dangerous in the slightest. But the message she sent was clear.

Zinnie gave her a sheepish look. She shrugged. "You do what you gotta do, you know? I don't make the rules around here."

The groan of the front door of the building as it opened interrupted Zinnie's argument with Lela.

Or with herself? No. With Lela. The dragon was speaking to her… in a way. Right?

Lela zipped to Zinnie's shoulder and tucked herself beneath her ear. Zinnie's long hair usually hid the dragon, but this shorter style did little to conceal her.

Zinnie pinched her own lips closed to force herself to remain quiet. Her mistress didn't use the front door to their space very often. It was more likely another of Mistress's "employees." Or a customer.

Chapter 4

*I*f there's one thing a thief is good at," Zinnie whispered to Lela, "it's sneaking around. Even if that sneaking is done in her own home."

Zinnie tiptoed into the hall and planted herself outside the door to the pawnbroker's shop that her mistress owned and operated. She leaned close, careful not to touch it, *almost* pressing her ear against the thin wood.

Using her acute observation skills that her mistress herself had taught her, she eavesdropped on the happenings on the other side of the door.

Two sets of footsteps.

A light pair coming from the far corner of the shop, where precarious stacks of books collected dust. That would be her mistress.

A second, heavier pair from the direction of the entrance.

"It is done," a man's rough voice grumbled.

"Very well. Any complications?" Her mistress's voice pierced the quiet like a knife.

Zinnie could just imagine the sharp look

from her mistress's dark brown eyes and the sneer that showed off her blinding teeth. It would be enough to put anyone in their place, no matter how burly or dangerous they may appear.

"No, ma'am." Just as Zinnie thought. Submissive. "All went as planned."

The man's next words were muffled by his shifting feet.

Zinnie frowned. It was none of her business what her mistress hired others to do. She was the only one who lived here, she reminded herself. Who was treated as if she was important.

Light footsteps crossed the space, then returned. Coins clinked inside a pouch. Her mistress paid him well for whatever he had done. It must have been an important job.

Zinnie did not get paid for her work. She was informed that her services were in exchange for room and board, as well as the careful upbringing she had received after her parents' untimely deaths.

The female voice was low and stern. "Speak of this to no one. Do *not* contact me again."

The image of her mistress's dark curls tossed over her shoulder and down her back, and her mistress's chin jutting forward entered Zinnie's imagination.

Why would she hire someone for a one-time job? That seemed like an awful waste of resources.

The man exited the shop with another ear-splitting metallic scrape of the door hinges.

Zinnie had oiled the hardware once. And had been harshly punished. Apparently, it was good to have a noisy door. As Zinnie became more accustomed to sneaking around, she agreed. She had overheard many things because of that squeaky door.

Zinnie was about to slip back to her room when the door screeched opened again.

She could picture in her mind's eye the hungry look on

her mistress's face at the prospect of a new customer. Or victim, as Zinnie understood them to be.

Her mistress greeted her new customer.

The reply startled Zinnie so much that she almost made the same mistake she had made the previous night. She willed her body to remain stiff so she wouldn't accidentally bang the door and alert anyone to her presence.

"Hello, Jessamine." The voice that spoke her mistress's name was soft, calm, yet not submissive like the man's voice had been.

Mistress Jessamine remained silent for several beats.

Whoever this was had caught Zinnie's mistress off guard. *Really* off guard. That was difficult to do.

She leaned closer to the door. She really wanted to open it to get a good look at whoever this person was, but that would be a big mistake. She must settle for eavesdropping, not truly spying.

The other woman spoke again. "It looks like you have done well for yourself."

If she only knew. Mistress Jessamine had done more than well for herself. She practically ruled the entire city with all the scheming and blackmailing and double crossing she did. It was just, no one seemed to notice.

Zinnie forced herself to refocus on the conversation.

"What are you doing here, Juliette?" Jessamine's voice dripped with contempt.

Juliette? Zinnie mouthed the name.

Lela purred into her ear. Zinnie ignored the dragon and continued to eavesdrop.

The woman replied in a measured tone. Like she was hiding something. "I have searched for you far and wide. I did not expect to find you... here."

Jessamine had been in the City of Dorian for decades as far as Zinnie could tell. How far and wide was the world if it took this Juliette woman ages to find her here?

"The best place to hide is in the middle of nowhere, in the middle of everything." Venom trickled from Jessamine's words. Zinnie could imagine the cold gaze that the other woman would be receiving right at that moment.

"Jessamine... you do not have to stay here. No one else knows what you have done. Everyone has assumed that Peter fled to avoid the marriage to Amelie. It's been long enough. It is all over. I have come to ask you..." the woman hesitated.

In that moment, Zinnie was eternally grateful for her nearly perfect recall. Otherwise, she would have needed to write down this exchange.

It was strange. And alarming. Mistress Jessamine treated everyone as if she was their superior. As if she had nothing to hide. But she, in fact, seemed to be hiding from the world. And who were Peter and Amelie?

Jessamine let out an exasperated sigh. "*What*, Juliette? What could you possibly want from me anymore?"

"Please," the woman begged. "Come home with me."

Zinnie's heart stuttered. *Come home?* Home... where? Would Mistress Jessamine go with this woman? What would that mean for Zinnie? Would she be released from her servitude?

She held her breath to await Jessamine's response.

"It's too late."

Zinnie's heart sank.

"That bridge is burned. It's nothing but ashes now." Jessamine's voice was hard as stone.

"It does not have to remain that way," the woman pleaded. She sounded like she was going to burst into tears at any second.

Mistress Jessamine was not sympathetic to tears. Zinnie learned that a long time ago. She hadn't shed a single tear in years.

The woman continued. "There is still a place for you."

Zinnie knew it would be foolish to hope that this person could somehow change Jessamine's mind about staying. It would be too good to be true…

"It IS that way, Juliette."

Zinnie flinched at the harshness of her mistress's response. That wasn't just a '*no*.' That was a threat. Zinnie gulped. This woman better be careful.

Mistress Jessamine spoke again. "You can't change what happened. You can't bring back my parents. Or Peter. It's over. I've moved on."

Zinnie felt like she had been struck. *Mistress Jessamine was an orphan, too?* Zinnie's thoughts clouded.

She shook her head to regain her focus. She would have to tuck that away for later pondering or else she might miss something important.

"What has become of you?" The other woman was crying. "Please, do not be this way, Jessamine."

"Stop." Would Mistress Jessamine do something to harm the woman?

Should Zinnie intervene? She placed her hand lightly on the door. She didn't know what she would do, but she readied herself, just in case.

Juliette did not heed the command. "Please do not let your heart become destroyed."

A silent pause stretched uncomfortably long.

Zinnie's hand trembled against the door. Her heart raced.

"Jessamine?" Juliette's voice came out as a squeak.

Would her mistress force the woman way? Would she lash out? Yell? Throw things, break things, like she did when she was really angry?

The words Jessamine spoke next were low. Flat. Unemotional. "If my heart has become as cinder, so be it."

The other woman, Juliette, sucked in a sharp breath.

Mistress Jessamine's words must have hurt worse than an actual blow would have.

The door creaked open and closed again.

The building was empty now except for Jessamine and Zinnie.

Zinnie remained planted in place. Her mind raced with the excessive amount of vague information she had overheard. What was she to do with it all? If only she had someone to talk to. Someone who could *actually* answer her questions, mull over ideas. She needed to go for a walk to sort it all out.

But the sounds that came from Jessamine on the other side of the door kept Zinnie from moving.

Chapter 5

Something crashed to the floor. Glass shattered into what sounded like a million pieces. The suddenness of it startled Zinnie. She stiffened. Leaned her ear closer to the door.

Mistress Jessamine let out a growl reminiscent of the rumored wolf-men that wandered the deep forests.

A cacophony of smashes, bangs, and breaks moved Zinnie away from the door.

The large raven that perched in the corner of the shop, untethered, squawked loudly.

"I know!" Jessamine shouted harshly back at the bird. "But I didn't expect to ever see… *her*… again!"

Another crash. Another squawk.

Jessamine grumbled, quieter this time, something about a map in a firmer voice than Zinnie had ever heard before.

Zinnie could only imagine the

destruction her Mistress caused in her own shop. As much as she wanted to know more about what happened, she didn't think it was a good idea to stick around and risk incurring that kind of wrath on herself. Who knew how her Mistress would take it out on her?

But if she didn't produce the fruits of her earlier job, it would only make things worse.

"Let's get this over with, Lela," she whispered.

She slipped back to her room, snatched the satchel off her bed, and hurried back toward her mistress.

She stopped right outside the door to the shop.

All was quiet on the other side. Would Jessamine lash out at her? Would the fact that she retrieved the thing her mistress wanted be enough to appease her anger?

Zinnie took a deep breath, held it for a few counts, then released it. She put a modest smile on her face and pushed the door open.

Mistress Jessamine stood in front of the raven as tall as Zinnie's torso. She stroked the feathers and spoke in low tones to the bird.

Zinnie didn't want to startle Mistress Jessamine, so she cleared her throat.

Jessamine pinned hard eyes on Zinnie over her shoulder, said something else to the bird, and turned around.

The bird flapped its oversized wings and flew out the partially opened dingy window.

Lela fluffed her feathers beneath Zinnie's hair and dug her claws into Zinnie's shoulder.

Zinnie begged the dragon to remain calm in her mind. Hopefully Lela would feel the sentiment.

Jessamine smoothed her expression into a neutral one and strode across the shop to Zinnie. "It's about time you returned," Jessamine scolded. "You really should learn to be more punctual. Did you acquire it?"

Zinnie nodded and reached inside her bag.

"Was there any trouble?" Jessamine kept a careful eye on Zinnie as she reached for the jars.

"No, Mistress." Zinnie dipped her head and kept her eyes on the floor. There was no way she was going to admit that she had nearly been caught because of a tiny manticore kitten. She also wasn't about to divulge the fact that she had kind of sort of *paid* for the items she had been tasked to steal.

Zinnie peeked at Jessamine and instantly noticed the suspicious look in her eyes. It took everything Zinnie had not to blush, or gulp, or flick her eyes away. Those tells would surely get her into trouble.

Jessamine inspected the contents of the bottles that Zinnie had… stolen. She gave a satisfied click of her tongue and placed the bottles on her counter off to one side.

"Did you have a customer?" Zinnie kept her voice steady, and innocent. She slouched her posture and fidgeted with her hands to give herself a more youthful appearance.

Mistress Jessamine's back stiffened. She quickly composed herself.

"No one of any importance to someone of *your* station." Her voice was muffled from facing away from Zinnie.

Something inside Zinnie wilted. She always hoped that when she had done her job well, Mistress Jessamine would express appreciation. Treat her more like a friend instead of an employee. The woman had told her since she was young that she cared about Zinnie, otherwise why would she have taken her in? But her actions never matched her words.

It was foolish to hope that Mistress Jessamine would ever see her as anything other than an asset, but Zinnie wanted a family more than anything. *Any* family. However small. She should know better than to let her guard down to hope for anything from Jessamine.

She didn't notice that her Mistress had turned around. She must have forgotten to hide her emotions with her usual mask, because the woman placed a finger beneath her chin and lifted it ever so slightly so that Zinnie would make eye contact.

"You worry too much, little girl." Jessamine looked into her eyes a little too long for Zinnie's comfort.

It made her squirm on the inside.

Jessamine broke eye contact and quickly pushed past Zinnie to the back of the shop. "We'll have everything we need soon enough. Then we will no longer want for anything. You'll see."

"Yes, Mistress." Zinnie's voice was barely above a whisper.

Considering the only thing she really wanted was a family… or her freedom, she doubted that whatever Jessamine had in mind would be satisfying for Zinnie.

Her heart twinged at the thought of abandoning the only home she had ever known, but nothing about her life was under her control. And as much as Jessamine pretended to be a mother figure to Zinnie, the truth was, Zinnie was just another pawn in Jessamine's games. She would give almost anything for something to change.

"…clean up this mess, then head out for your errands. Are you listening to me?"

Zinnie snapped her attention back to Jessamine. "Of course." She bobbed her head. "You were giving me my chores for the day."

She *hadn't* been listening, but it wasn't difficult to guess what her mistress expected from her. It was much the same every day. The only difference was that Zinnie would clean up the mess that Jessamine had made in her shop before she could do her errands. She'd have to work fast in order to get it all done and still have time for herself.

"… and make sure you bring back something *good* today for a change, do you understand?"

"Yes, ma'am."

Zinnie retrieved the broom from the corner and started by sweeping the broken shards of ceramic from the floor. The remains of the bizarre idol from some far-off land filled the dustpan. It was a strange piece that one of Jessamine's customers had pawned. Those customers seldom returned for their "treasured" items.

She stacked the books that had been knocked to the floor in Jessamine's tirade and placed them back onto the shelf. She had always wanted to organize the shelf by color or size or something, but she had never taken the time to do it. Some of the thicker volumes weighed more than Zinnie could easily heft, but she managed to hoist them onto the bottom shelf. She brushed the dust from her palms.

She righted the barrel of weapons and arranged the tridents, maces, and swords in a bouquet of spikes, points, and blades of unusual workmanship.

The shelf with the shed dragon claws and harvested scales had tipped, and she straightened it and replaced the contents in as pleasing an arrangement as she could.

Finally, Zinnie straightened the messy piles of discarded armor pieces, swept the entire floor of the shop, and made sure nothing would be found out of place. Jessamine had as sharp of a memory as Zinnie and would notice anything missing or askew.

Once she was sure everything was as perfect as a disorderly pawn shop could be, she returned the broom to the corner, took one last look around, and set out into the city for the day.

Lela rested on Zinnie's shoulder as she wandered through the crowded market near the city gates. That's where it was easiest to choose new marks. The people there were travelers, or new to the city.

The market offered the perfect distraction and the size of

the crowd allowed Zinnie to appear and disappear with ease. Her short height, preteen appearance, and disguised body underneath the lavender satin clothing disarmed people. Her innocent smile pushed them to trust her. Her pretty little dragon charmed women and children. The use of "Sir" and "Ma'am" elicited trust.

She didn't know what kind of items she would bring home from today's excursion, but she knew how to start the hunt.

She removed a gaudy faux pearl bracelet from her pocket, waited for just the right moment, and dropped it at the feet of an unsuspecting victim. She continued her stroll, keeping an eye on her mark from the corner of her eye.

Lela skittered up and down her arm, attracting the gaze of a handful of children who crowded around her to see her pet up close. Crouched with children around her and her own bright smile and kind eyes encouraged the mark to return the misplaced bracelet to the sweet girl who had dropped it.

Lela distracted the children by flying circles overhead. The mark observed with a joyful expression on his face. And Zinnie slipped the man's own pocket watch from his vest without him being any the wiser.

A twinge of guilt pierced her, but she brushed it away and told herself that she did what she must to survive.

As she perused the shops around the perimeter of the market, she held doors for women and children, and as the mothers bustled their offspring through, she would slip a purse or hair pin from them without them noticing.

She tripped in front of a cart, forcing someone to rescue her. And allowing her to pick their pockets, too.

If the item proved to be of little value, she often slipped it back without the person even being aware of its absence in the first place.

After her narrow escape that morning in the apothecary shop, she felt invincible. Light on her feet. Able to pull off the impossible. She shared her edible prizes with beggar children hiding in the shadows, and even offered them a piece of jewelry to pawn for money that should last them a week.

She had to believe that if she returned home with the right item, then maybe Mistress Jessamine's heart would soften, and she would show the tiniest bit of warmth toward Zinnie.

In the back of her mind, she knew it would never be true. Otherwise, Mistress Jessamine would have found a way to lift the enchantment that kept Zinnie inside the city. The enchantment that had been placed upon her before she could even remember.

Jessamine had done exactly the opposite. She reminded Zinnie of her troubled past and unfortunate curse as often as possible.

38

Chapter 6

Zinnie's parents had stolen something valuable from the wrong person. When their deceit had been discovered, a curse had been placed upon them.

And their toddling child.

"Remember," Jessamine liked to remind Zinnie, "no matter how hard you try, you will never be able to leave the City of Dorian. Just be grateful that I had the compassion to take the cursed orphan child into my own home and raise you like family." The sentiment was often accompanied by a condescending pat on the head or a harsh click of the tongue.

A few years back, Zinnie had tested Jessamine's words, sure that her mistress had lied to her to manipulate her to stay. She had witnessed it happen to so many others, that the doubt had seeped in over time.

But when she tried to cross the threshold of the city, it had been like walking right into the massive wall that surrounded the entire city. She pushed against the invisible barrier with her hands, her shoulder. But to no avail. The walls of the city might as well stretch solid right across the main road that led out of the City of Dorian.

Frustrated, preteen Zinnie had tried climbing the wall. It had worked. Until she got to the top. The invisible barrier prevented her from crossing over the top to descend the other side.

Just as Jessamine said, she was truly trapped in the City of Dorian. Her own personal prison poised precariously over the Dorian Sea.

"You really shouldn't complain, child," Jessamine had scolded her once. "At least you aren't confined to one of the actual prison towers. At least you are allowed freedom of movement, even if you cannot leave the city."

Jessamine fed her and provided her with all of her necessities. Zinnie had always done exactly as she was told in order to ease her guilt about the burden she had been on Jessamine since her youth.

But since trying to escape those few times, the desire to leave the city had grown. Zinnie wanted nothing more than to leave, to taste freedom. Find her own way in the vast world of Tala that she had only read about in books and heard rumors about from the travelers into the city.

She had vowed to herself that one day she would no longer be under Jessamine's care. No longer bound to the City of Dorian that had gradually closed in around her. She would find a way.

"You dropped this." A smooth voice came from behind.

Of course, she dropped her glowing white handkerchief. That was the whole idea. She put on an innocent face and turned to discover who her next mark would be.

Her cornflower blue eyes met the steely gray gaze of a handsome face. A *young* handsome face.

A flutter erupted in her stomach. Hummingbird wings.

Probably just grumbling for lunch…

Lela returned to hide beneath her hair, now grown to a little past her shoulders. The dragon's tiny claws on Zinnie's neck tickled. Which would explain the small shiver that ran down her spine at the exact moment that the boy in front of her gave her a sincere smile. It showed off the shallow dimples in his cheeks.

He ran his fingers through his shiny black, messy hair. Leaving it in even more disarray on his head. His other hand still outstretched holding Zinnie's embroidered handkerchief.

She swallowed and retrieved the lacy fabric. She dipped her head and dropped her gaze.

"Thank you," she whispered in a voice pitched a little higher than her natural tone.

She looked up at him again. Her head just reached his shoulder.

Dark stubble dotted his chin and jaw line. For how round and soft her own features were, lending her the air of youth, his features were all sharp angles and lines. But his eyes exuded kindness. And his smile…

She shook her head. She was supposed to be evaluating where he may be holding his valuables. Looking for jewelry or time pieces that she might be able to swipe without him noticing. Not getting caught up in his handsome features and stunning smile.

"*Atlas!*" A man's voice called from down the street.

He whipped his head around. "Coming, Father!"

He returned his gaze to Zinnie, dipped his own head, and said, "Have a nice day, miss! Don't lose your handkerchief again!"

Atlas turned on his heels and jogged down the street to his father's side. They walked along beside a small carriage and a wagon pulling belongings. Moving to the city by the looks of it. A woman and a girl sat on the bench of the carriage. Probably his mother and sister.

Before long they were lost in the crowd and Zinnie found herself staring dumbly after them.

What had come over her? Why had she reacted that way to that boy? Sure, he was handsome. And kind for returning her handkerchief. But that had never stopped her from following through on a mark before. What had happened?

A bell rang from one of the towers that surrounded the city. It snapped Zinnie out of her head. Her stomach fluttered again.

Probably just hungry. "I'd better find some food."

Zinnie watched Mistress Jessamine's face carefully when she presented her with the items she had retrieved during her "errands."

"Another potion? Really, child. You can be such a disappointment."

Jessamine picked over the other items with a frown.

Zinnie imbued confidence into her voice but kept her excitement to a minimum. "It's not just any potion." She pulled the woman's attention back to the "disappointing" item. "It's sap from a dragon tree…"

Jessamine turned her dark eyes onto Zinnie and nodded once. "That will do." She placed the potion bottle in one of her deep pockets on the side of her simple dress. "Now, change out of those ridiculous clothes and prepare for supper. You look foolish wearing such an unbecoming outfit." She marched through the door to the kitchen without a backward glance at Zinnie.

Zinnie wilted. She had hoped for at least a little praise. The youthful appearance that projected vulnerability did not work on her mistress.

Staring at her warped reflection in the mirror, she sighed. "What am I going to do, Lela? I feel so trapped, like one of those caged animals at the palace menagerie."

Lela shuddered from her perch atop the mirror.

"Sorry." Zinnie stroked Lela's iridescent feathers.

Lela had escaped from the menagerie a couple of years ago. She did not like to be reminded of her time there.

"But it's nice to know that at least someone knows how I feel." She tickled the dragon under her chin.

Lela stretched her wings and fluffed her feathers.

"Exactly," Zinnie answered.

Zinnie turned her head from side to side to examine her now waist length locks. "I think I'll wait until morning to cut it."

With her hair expertly weaved into a mass of various sized braids, she tied them all together at the bottom with a leather cord. She hung the lavender dress on one of the hooks by her door and removed the binding from her chest.

The hunter green, soft canvas sheath dress she wore instead fit comfortably over Zinnie's slight frame, and with the laces on the sides cinched the garment shaped nicely to her body. She wore a pale cotton half-sleeved blouse beneath the dress and made sure the deep pockets on either side had nothing hiding in them.

"Now I feel like myself again," Zinnie sighed.

She glanced at Lela preening atop the mirror. "You coming?"

The dragon flapped her wings and hovered in the air and swooped low to land on Zinnie's arm. She scurried up to take her place on her shoulder.

"A new family has moved into town," Zinnie said between bites of her bland stew.

Zinnie wondered again why they ate such basic food all the time. Mistress Jessamine must be wealthy with all the blackmails and stealing she provided to the less savory characters within the city. But she certainly didn't live like it. Was trying to hide her wealth from others, to extract pity and charity? Or did she spend all the money on something that Zinnie was not aware of instead of providing herself and Zinnie with better food?

Jessamine took a bite of her own stew and stared at Zinnie, waiting for further information about the new family Zinnie had mentioned.

Chapter 7

As much as Zinnie would have liked to hear questions like, "How was your day?" or "Did you make any new friends?" their conversations sounded more like "What did you bring me?" or "What useful information did you discover?"

Zinnie swallowed and tried to remain business-like, even though she pretended their conversation was about boys or Zinnie's future instead of the potential new mark for Jessamine. "They appeared to be quite wealthy. They could have expensive items that have gone 'missing' during their journey…"

Zinnie took another bite of her stew and waited for her mistress's reaction.

Jessamine paused mid-bite and cocked her head. "Tell me more about this family. What did you learn of them?"

Zinnie almost choked. *Why had she brought them up?* She didn't know *anything* about them and that would only annoy her mistress. She racked her precise memory for any information that could be useful.

"Their clothing was well-tailored.

They had a handful of servants attending them, though the father appeared to drive his own carriage. Their wagon of belongings was heavy laden, pulled by two oxen through the crowded street."

Jessamine chewed slowly. "Anything else?"

"The teenage son's name is Atlas?" Zinnie hoped it would be useful information, though she didn't know how.

Jessamine paused. A look of intrigue crossed her dark features. "Learn more about this family. Everything you can. Tomorrow. Then report back to me as soon as you discover anything useful."

Zinnie dropped her gaze to her bowl. "Yes ma'am." She was so tired of uttering those words. What she wouldn't give for a "thank you" at least some of the time.

The way Jessamine interacted with her wealthier clients portrayed the picture of warmth and kindness. Her smooth olive skin and sleek dark curls betrayed the fact that she had lived for a very long time. Her exact age was a mystery.

But she never behaved like that at home. Zinnie would even settle for *fake* affection if that's all she could get. Jessamine had never shown her anything of the sort.

Zinnie wore her green dress again the following morning after she cut her hair short and added the locks to the case beneath the bed. She needed information, and the bustling market dressed as an innocent girl would not be the place to find it. She would need to explore the darker, edgier parts of the city.

She weaved her way down the maze of cobblestone, through dark alleys, and under precarious walkways that connected some of the buildings to one another.

She avoided the wood nymphs that clustered together inside the sprawling park that had a slow-moving stream running through it. They would never reduce themselves to speaking with a lowly working orphan like Zinnie, only reserving their slow speech and vast knowledge to those of much higher standing.

The messenger fawns, with their goat legs and youthful human upper bodies, were always in too much of a hurry to stop to talk to anyone. Zinnie had tried a number of times. They saw much of the city and interacted with all kinds of people. Just like Zinnie. But they were also skittish. The only time she had managed to get one to speak with her was when she gifted him a crimson scarf to wrap around his neck on a chilly wet day. Still, he hadn't disclosed much of anything, insisting that part of his job was to keep secrets.

Zinnie was supposed to keep secrets, too. And she did, for the most part. Sometimes, though, she would trade information if it wouldn't end up causing harm to someone. Especially an innocent someone.

The bushy-bearded dwarves, however, had no such reservations. They were always good for information as long as she had the right trinket to exchange. She wondered how accurate their knowledge really was. But had concluded long ago that even less-than-accurate information proved better than none at all.

Beneath her skirts, her purse bumped against her hip. It carried a small selection of low-end jewelry, a handful of coins from far-off lands, a packet of golden dorma flower pollen, and a book of charms that may or may not have been totally fabricated by a leprechaun. The right prize offered to the right person would allow her to learn what she needed to know.

She also carried a trove of knowledge in her memory: upcoming shipments of smuggled items or animals, names of contacts that could be useful for disreputable purposes, current whereabouts of certain of the city leaders… and if she didn't have the knowledge that informant wished to trade for, she could find it.

Her first stop of the day would be at the inn. More specifically, the dining room at the inn. This wasn't the sort of establishment where she could just walk through and ask people what she wanted to know, though. She would have to blend in.

She had an understanding with the innkeeper that she could serve customers as long as she gave him any tips she earned. That way she could chat people up, eavesdrop, and find out what she wanted to know, and the innkeeper would receive extra income.

After a shift in the dining room, and a quick bite from the inn's kitchen of a baked potato and mug of hot cider, she joined the servants in the washroom. Again, free work resulted in free information. The gossip of the staff offered even more knowledge than just what she wanted to know about the new family in the city.

She ran errands for the innkeeper at the central market where the servants for the city leaders were likely to shop and gossip as well.

The more information she gathered, the closer she got to her target, eventually discovering the truth of this new family.

"They're from Elodale, all the way across Tala." Zinnie reported back to Jessamine at the end of the day. "They are quite wealthy and have been pursued by the city leaders to come to Dorian. They have taken up the Barlowe mansion near the palace."

When Zinnie had learned that the family lived near the palace, she had been frustrated. That place was guarded by gargoyles that even Zinnie dared not mess with. The city leaders, not royalty by any stretch of the imagination even though they liked to pretend they were, kept their palace, and their secrets, well-guarded. It would be a difficult place to infiltrate if Jessamine ended up assigning Zinnie with that task. She could do it, though, if she had to.

Jessamine pulled Zinnie back to the conversation. "And what is the purpose of the family for being here? Why did the leaders send for them and why are they keeping them close?" Jessamine feigned disinterest. But she seldom asked questions like these. Her curiosity was certainly piqued.

Zinnie's had been, too. That's why she had spent the last couple hours of the day observing the family for herself.

"The father, Gentleman Forster, I believe, is rumored to be one of the best mapmakers across Tala."

Jessamine's eyes snapped to Zinnie's face. She covered it up by brushing a stray brown lock from her cheek and picking up her bonepen with her other. She pretended to be balancing her ledger. Misdirection. Distraction.

But she had taught Zinnie those skills well, and now Zinnie knew when she was being deceived.

Jessamine spoke with measured calmness. "And what of the family themselves? Did you spend time observing them?"

Zinnie's heart sank. In the time spent observing them, she had learned much about these people.

The parents behaved with kindness toward their servants and staff. Atlas played with his younger sister. He clearly loved her. He also helped out where he could with the tasks at hand. All four of them wore smiles on their faces and laughed freely with one another.

Jealousy had pricked Zinnie's heart like a thorn. It was the perfect family life she had always dreamed of for herself.

"There are two parents, the son- Atlas, and a younger sister. They had their servants unload a large number of belongings into the Barlowe mansion. It would appear they plan to stay for a long time." Zinnie kept her other observations about the nature of their character to herself.

Jessamine pinched her lips and lowered her eyebrows. "How many servants?"

Why did Jessamine wish to know this information? A pit

formed in Zinnie's stomach. Guilt trickled down her spine. Had she divulged too much? What did Jessamine want with this family? With this mapmaker?

She chose her words carefully. "They only brought a handful of servants with them,"

"They will need to hire others from the city to assist in settling in," Jessamine murmured to herself. A calculating expression clouded her eyes.

Zinnie's practiced firm posture hid her surprise from showing when Jessamine blurted her next words.

"I have a new job for you. You will infiltrate their cleaning staff and report back every detail about what you see and hear inside their home." She murmured to herself again. "This may be just the thing I've been hoping for."

Zinnie didn't immediately respond with "Yes, ma'am" like usual.

Jessamine pinned her with a pointed stare. "Is there a problem?" She lifted one eyebrow and peered down her nose at Zinnie.

What could Zinnie say?

She didn't want to deceive this perfect family. They genuinely seemed like great people. The city could use more kindness and goodness. Why did Jessamine have to take advantage of the good people that made their way here every time? It only drove them away and left the city a darker, lonelier place than it had been before.

Jessamine's calculated voice prodded. "Need I remind you that I made a promise to your parents to look after you? And isn't that what I have done? I have provided you with the best education and a home."

Zinnie nodded. "I know."

"It's not like you would have had such a life with your parents if they hadn't died so suddenly. Who knows where you would have been? What you would have been forced to do?"

Zinnie found that statement ironic since her mistress had made her do many things she had not wanted to do.

And even though she knew little about its origins, she had that stupid enchantment that forbade her from leaving Dorian. She likely would have ended up as a street urchin like so many other orphans in the city.

In a way, Mistress Jessamine had kept her promise. She had provided Zinnie with a roof over her head and meals, even if they weren't tasty ones. She had also provided Zinnie with a level of education she would not have found otherwise.

Because of Jessamine, Zinnie learned all the fine arts that a proper woman should know. She had also learned all the not-so fine arts that a con-woman should know. She had spent time with the blacksmith as well as ladies of high society. Everyone owed Jessamine something, so they couldn't really question her when she requested they teach Zinnie everything they knew.

Now here she was, nearly an adult with a well-rounded skill set that would serve her in any number of situations. Including the one that Jessamine pressed onto her now.

"You *will* do this thing for me?" It was more of a command, though she made it sound like a question.

What choice did Zinnie really have? "Yes, ma'am."

"Very well. You will acquire the necessary supplies tonight before you go to bed and begin your job first thing in the morning." She looked Zinnie up and down. "And you may want to do something about that hair." She gave her a disgusted look.

Chapter 8

By the time Zinnie had acquired the clothing of a house maid and made the proper inquiries on how to get hired, the sun had long past dipped below the walls around the City of Dorian. She plopped onto her bed and fell into a deep sleep at once.

In the morning, her hair had grown past her ankles and dragged on the floor.

Zinnie sighed when she nearly tripped on it in her groggy state before sunup.

She hastily let out the braids and reweaved them to include the new growth. She carefully used her scissors to cut the braid off at the nape of her neck. She would hide her compact blond curls beneath her servant's cap when she went to Atlas's house.

Her stomach tightened. She wished she hadn't said anything about them to Jessamine.

But the woman would have discovered them eventually. At least this way Zinnie could guarantee their safety from some of Jessamine's rougher employees. She hoped.

"Sorry, Lela, you'll have to stay home today. We'll be near the palace, and I'll be working all day. I'll tell you everything when I return."

Lela let out a huff of smoke and blinked at Zinnie.

"Don't be mad. I promise we'll do something fun tomorrow."

Lela stared at her.

"You're right. I can't make that kind of promise. But I can promise to bring you back a treat, how does that sound?"

Lela twirled in a circle and curled into a feather ball again. Puffs of steam came from her nose as she settled back to sleep.

Fortunately, the other servants in the now-Forster mansion did not recognize Zinnie. They worked for the higher classes within Dorian, and Zinnie had not spent much time around any of them. Plus, with her blond curls hidden, they wouldn't recognize her even if they had seen her before.

Hired as a housemaid, Zinnie gathered her cleaning supplies and climbed the stairs to the top floor of the house to begin removing cobwebs, dusting furniture, and opening windows and curtains to air out the long-unlived-in home.

Being the floor that housed servants, this floor had small rooms, narrow halls, and little adornments to reflect the wealth of the family who lived here. The steeply pitched roofs left the ceilings low around the perimeter. The turrets attached to the corners of the homes, though they looked real, were there simply for show and not accessible.

If Zinnie ever had a home like this, which was laughable at best, she would make sure the turrets could be entered and had stairs inside. What a perfect observation spot to be able to see everything around you!

At the front of the third floor, Zinnie cleaned out the fireplace in what would be a nursery if the family had young children. The Forster's did not, so this room would likely remain unused.

"What a waste…" Zinnie mumbled to herself. The room spread ten times larger than her own tiny room. What she wouldn't give to live in a place like this!

She *could* leave Jessamine and become a servant like she pretended to be today. But that life would quickly become dull. At least the life she lived now allowed for variety and adventure. Even if the adventure never extended beyond the walls of Dorian.

The second floor of the house exhibited the wealth of the family. The ceiling stretched twice as high as Zinnie. Ornate wallpaper textured with velvet designs covered the walls. The other walls that had only paint on them boasted deep shades of burgundy and eggplant.

Each room Zinnie entered brightened as soon as she flung open the rich curtains. The light reflected off shiny surfaces of highly polished wood furniture pieces. The bedrooms of the family lined one side of the wide, plush-carpeted hallway. The other side held a library, study, and sitting room for more intimate family gatherings.

"If there are maps here, they'd be in the study," Zinnie whispered as she dusted the mahogany chair rail along the length of the hallway.

She approached the door to the study and pushed it open. The room contained fine furniture, heavy curtains, flowery wallpaper, and thick rugs covering much of the hardwood floor. A stack of paintings, still wrapped in paper for travel, leaned against the wall beside the door.

The shelves of the built-in bookcases had already been cleaned, and the windows and ceiling swept for dust and cobwebs.

"Drat. I'll have no excuse for staying in here… Another time, I suppose." Zinnie carefully closed the door. Her hand brushed the unique ironwork handle. She bent to get a closer look.

"Well, this is different," she said to herself. She examined the peculiar lock that had been recently added to the door. "Did Gentleman Forster install this himself?"

"Less dilly-dallying, more workin'," the head maid scolded Zinnie as she carried a basket of folded laundry to one of the bedrooms on the floor.

"Yes, ma'am," slipped from Zinnie's lips out of habit.

She descended the stairs, mind still focused on the strange lock. If she was tasked to break into that room, it might be a problem.

"No, a challenge," she reminded herself. "Besides, who's to say that will even be necessary?"

But she knew she was only kidding herself. Jessamine had seemed very interested in the *mapmaking* detail about the Forster family. It was only a matter of time before Zinnie would find herself here again, she was sure.

The first floor of the home had been updated with all the latest gadgets- gas lighting, water pumps in the scullery at the back of the house, and even an indoor toilet that had the waste removed by pipes that led to underground sewers.

The drawing room, parlor, dining hall, and additional library all matched the rest of the first and second floors. Rich colors, expensive gold-tasseled upholstery, highly intricate rare wood furniture, decorated frames around enormous works of art. Even house plants and garlands that framed ornate tapestries.

"This all seems a bit… much." Zinnie balked at the extravagance of it all. "How many orphans and widows could be cared for at the price of just one of these items…"

The wheels in her head began to turn, but she forced herself to remain focused on the task at hand.

She had a good handle on the home. Now she needed to understand more about the servants and family who lived in it.

The cellar below the scullery and beside the kitchen would be the perfect place to start.

"I heard that Miss Lucy is treated as a princess by her father," one scullery made said as she stirred the enormous pot of boiling water. Steam left water droplets on every surface of her hair and skin.

"With hair the color of bronze and that perfect pouty smile, I can see why," another woman said as she pressed a hot iron onto a large tablecloth to smooth out the wrinkles.

Zinnie carried a basket of bedsheets to the pot of boiling water. She hefted it over the side and dumped the contents into the water. Sweat trickled down her temples and dripped into one of her eyes. She hissed at the stinging sensation. This was why she would rather live alone with Jessamine than work in a house as a servant.

"The Forster boy- what was his name again?- he sure is handsome." The girl stirring the hot cloth giggled.

The others joined her. Zinnie played along.

"What do you make of Gentlewoman Forster as a mistress?" A woman folded the freshly smoothed bedsheets and placed them into a basket below the table.

"I hear she's a dream to work for. Actually says 'thank you' and 'please.' Allows the maids time off to spend with family. I hope they stay here for ever and ever. I'll never want to leave!" Stirring Girl beamed with her praise.

Just as Zinnie thought. Good people who didn't deserve to be the target of Jessamine. For any reason.

The scent of mutton, yeast, and sweets wafted in when another servant entered the scullery. Zinnie's stomach growled. She could use some of Gentlewoman Forster's generosity right about now.

But she didn't have time for food. She had to find out everything she could. The end of the day fast approached.

"Take this to the second floor," Folding Lady said to Ironing Girl.

"I'll do it," Zinnie piped up. She hurried to grab the basket.

The woman holding the hot iron shrugged. "If you insist. I don't wish to climb those stairs again today!"

Zinnie placed the folded sheets on the bed inside one of the rooms. A peek into the closet revealed day dresses and modest evening clothes.

"This must be Lucy's room…"

Heavy footsteps plodded up the stairs. She couldn't be caught lingering. She picked up the basket and rushed out the bedroom door.

"Oh!" she cried as she collided with none other than Gentleman Forster himself.

He had thick brown hair, a trimmed beard, and shining gray eyes. "Pardon me, Miss!"

He actually apologized to her. She should be groveling at his feet!

She dropped her gaze to the floor and curtsied. "No, my apologies. I shall be more careful next time."

"Father, is everything alright?" Atlas stepped out of the adjacent room to Lucy's.

Zinnie sucked in a sharp breath. She curtsied to Gentleman Forster again and darted for the stairs.

What if Atlas had recognized her? She couldn't risk him seeing that she was the same person as the "girl" in the street the other day.

She flew down the stairs, left the basket at the foot of them, and ran out the door at the back of the house.

She shoved her apron and bonnet in the bushes and made her way home as fast as she could.

It was ridiculous to think that anything would come of it if he recognized her, but she couldn't take any chances. She had a sinking feeling she would be forced to interact with him again.

Chapter 9

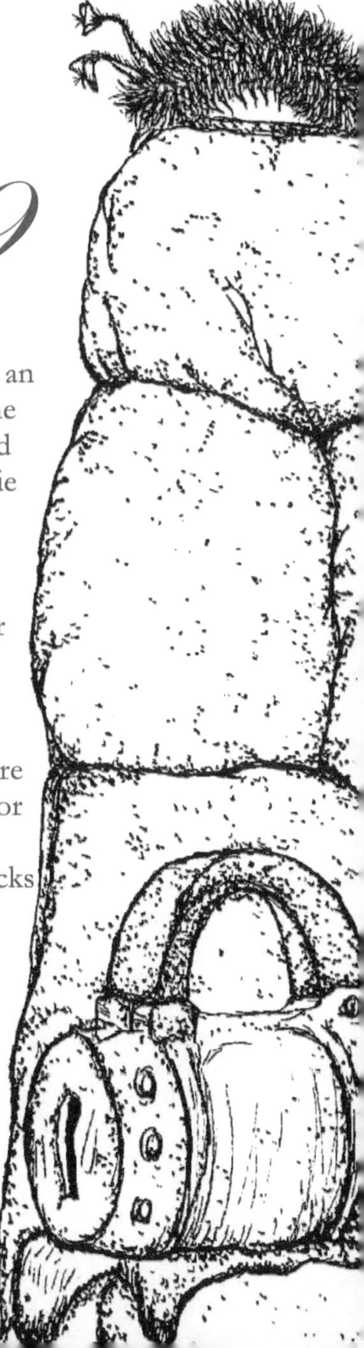

The head of the household has an extensive map collection in the library. The staff mostly talked about the mother and children." Zinnie forced her hands to remain still in her lap. She couldn't let Jessamine see her nerves.

Jessamine pinched her eyes and her lips. "How were the maps displayed?"

"Some hung on the walls in the library in frames. Many were part of large volumes of loose-leaf maps. There was a reading stand and a large table for examining them. Some weren't even unpacked and put away yet, still in stacks on the floor and chairs."

"What about an office or study?"

"The study door was locked." Zinnie maintained eye contact and kept her face neutral to avoid the detection of her lie.

Jessamine clicked her tongue. "That should not be a problem for a talented, dishonest person like you."

Zinnie swallowed. "It was a new kind of lock that I haven't seen before. I… I need time to figure it out…"

Jessamine heaved a deep sigh. "You have one week. Figure it out. Do not delay."

"Mistress… may I ask a question?" Zinnie kept her voice meek.

"I cannot guarantee I will answer you, but you may," Jessamine answered.

"Is there a… specific map you're looking for?"

"Who said I was looking for a map at all?" Jessamine folded her arms over her chest.

"Oh, um... I just assumed."

"Do not worry your little head over this. This is the answer to all of our troubles."

"Yes ma'am." The words came out without Zinnie even thinking about it.

The thing was, Zinnie's only real trouble was Mistress Jessamine. But maybe if she could do this one thing for Jessamine then her own troubles would be over, too. Maybe she could find a way to break the enchantment. Or maybe Jessamine would simply allow her to leave her employ.

If she was to succeed, she would need to plan carefully.

The first step would be to hire a trusted blacksmith to replicate the lock she had seen. No one in the City of Dorian could *really* be trusted, but there was one particular blacksmith that had under the table dealings with Jessamine that required him to work for her at a moment's notice, regardless of how much business he currently had waiting for him.

Zinnie showed him the drawings she had made after inspecting the lock and told him she needed it by the next day. Once she had that in hand, the real work could begin.

Since she had nothing else to do the rest of the day, she

hovered around the palace walls, avoiding the gargoyles that stood guard, and the others who gawked at the massive building.

Lela, who happily rode on her shoulder now, hissed in her ear like a reprimand.

"It's for the job," Zinnie insisted. She stood on tip toes and craned her neck to try to get a good look around. "I need to study their movements and habits so I can figure out the best way to get back into the house and pick the lock."

Lela pinched Zinnie's shoulder with her claws.

"What? It's true!"

Zinnie's heart leaped when she spotted Atlas making his way through the crowd. He was alone this time.

She couldn't help the grin that pulled at the corner of her cheeks at the sight of him. He sure was easy to look at, and the little she knew of his personality only made him all the more handsome.

Lela let out a spark that lightly scorched Zinnie's neck.

"What was that for?" she scolded her pet.

She looked at the crowd again. Atlas was headed right for her, his eyes focused straight ahead. Had he seen her? She should hide! What if he recognized her? Either as the young girl from his first day in the city, or as the maid that collided with his father in his own home just the day before? Both would be difficult to explain.

"Maybe that was my sister?" she said out loud, thinking of a quick excuse just in case.

But the girl in the market had been dressed expensively. Zinnie wore less exquisite clothing today.

"And what about yesterday?" Her mind raced.

Her hair was shoulder length today and hung loose around her face, but she hadn't done much else to disguise herself either then or now.

She dove behind a portly man who waddled along the wall

and gawked at the gargoyle that stood guard.

When Atlas drew level with her, she slipped around the man until his girth blocked her from the front.

She glanced over her shoulder, and the man's shoulder, which earned her a grunt and a glare from the fellow.

Atlas didn't slow down or look around. He hadn't spotted her. He was on some other errand that had nothing to do with her.

Of course he was. It was silly to think otherwise. She was sure he hadn't given her a second thought. She had been a thirteen-year-old girl the first time they had met, and yesterday she was a womanly servant with hair hidden beneath a cap. There was no reason to believe he would recognize her one way or another.

"What has gotten into you, Zinnie?" she scolded herself. "You can't let an attractive face distract you from what must be done."

She hovered around the Forster's home, but not too close, for the remainder of the day, until she returned to her own home to try to get a good night's sleep. She had a busy day of lock picking ahead of her.

Besides, you're just a girl with a talent for thievery. Atlas would never like a girl like you.

Practicing a new lock always worked better in natural light, but Zinnie didn't want anyone to see what she was doing or ask too many questions. And since her home had very little natural light, she had to find someplace secluded.

She settled at the top of one of the lookout towers along the protective wall of the city. The guards took shifts, and she had bribed one of them to leave for the afternoon so she could have some time alone. The man had taken the payment she offered and didn't even glance back when he tromped away.

Zinnie sat crisscrossed on the stone floor, the lock placed

in front of her and the tools in a precise semi-circle like sun rays coming out of the lock. She took a deep breath and got to work.

Lela perched on one of the higher sections of the ledge and cooed from time to time. Zinnie looked up to see what her friend reacted to. A flock of seabirds circled in the air beyond the wall before diving into the water below.

"You can go play, you know. Anytime you want..." Zinnie focused on the lock again while she spoke to her tiny, feathered friend.

Lela shot gray smoke from her mouth.

Zinnie still didn't look up. She puzzled over the lock, examining it carefully to make sure she got it right.

Lela swooped to land on one of Zinnie's knees. She looked up at Zinnie and blinked her long lashed, golden eyes at her. She made a purring sound.

Zinnie chuckled. "If you insist on staying with me, you might end up stuck here for a very long time." She returned her eyes to the lock.

"Maybe if I..." she murmured as she studied her project.

Lela landed on Zinnie's hand and pinched her thumb with her lips.

"I'm sure we'll figure out a way to escape eventually. But until then..." Zinnie frowned. Then she smiled. "I got it!"

Lela flew straight up and flapped her wings. She cooed again.

"Oh, no, Lela, not our escape. The lock. I know how to crack the lock. Or at least, I know how to figure out how to crack the lock. And I'll need a piece of wood about this thick." She held her thumb and pointer finger a little bit apart from one another. "It doesn't have to be very big... just bigger than this." She pointed at the lock.

Lela flew away to retrieve what Zinnie needed.

While Zinnie waited for Lela to return, she stood and

stretched her arms and legs. Then she, too, leaned against one of the waist-high sections of the wall.

She gazed out over the city. People looked like miniature versions of themselves from way up there. She laughed. "They all look like brownies!"

Her eyes followed a carriage through the city, and she watched when it stopped at the gate to the palace. The gargoyle hopped gracefully from its post like a lion and sniffed the entire outside of the carriage. It let out a gravely roar and nudged one wheel with its stone-like muzzle. One of its horns tore a hole in the side of the carriage.

The driver hastily turned the carriage around and retreated.

Zinnie chuckled to herself. People could be so arrogant to think they could make it past those things.

A head of messy black hair caught Zinnie's attention. She stood up a little straighter and leaned out a little further. Was it Atlas?

The man turned and she saw at once that it wasn't him.

Her heart sank.

She didn't have time to reflect on her reaction, because Lela returned right then with the requested piece of wood.

"Thanks, Lela." Zinnie looked at the man again, just in case, and confirmed it was a stranger. Then she returned to her lock.

With the lock secured to the wood the same way the one had been attached to the door at Atlas's house, she had a better time visualizing how to break it. It took longer than she expected, but, eventually, she figured it out.

By the time she finished, the afternoon had turned into evening. Zinnie's back was stiff from bending over the lock. Her backside was numb from sitting on the hard surface for so long. And her leg muscles were tight from staying in the same position for several hours.

Zinnie's stomach grumbled, reminding her that she hadn't eaten anything all day, either. She packed up her belongings, stashed the lock attached to the wood piece in one of her hiding places near the base of the wall, and made her way toward the central market.

She ate her hand pie wrapped in butcher paper and meandered through the market. When she spotted a hungry looking girl working at a vendor stand, she shared the pastry with her while she made small talk. The girl gave her a suspicious look, but Zinnie kept the conversation light and wished the girl a good evening when she left.

Zinnie's mind wandered, and she allowed her feet to carry her wherever they wanted. Lela remained perched on her shoulder.

Before she knew it, Zinnie found herself on the road that led toward Atlas's house. She didn't even realize where she was until she spotted the young man and his sister coming toward her.

Chapter 10

With her loose blonde curls tucked behind her ears, Zinnie ducked down a dark alley to observe the siblings as they passed. Atlas probably wouldn't recognize her, but she couldn't take any chances.

Lucy's bright laugh echoed off the crooked buildings. "No, Atlas. It's *sixteen*, not twenty-nine."

What were they doing down here? Usually, only servants roamed this part of the city.

Atlas's charming voice reached Zinnie's ears next. "No… my age, plus the distance between the towers, divided by the date, minus the number of people in our family equals… Oh. You're right. It's sixteen."

Lucy laughed again. Her face radiated joy. "Told you!"

Atlas smiled at her. He was head and shoulders taller than his younger sister. She had her hand nestled in the crook of his arm and she leaned against him. They looked so comfortable together.

He ruffled her hair. "I knew the answer,

I was testing you to see if you knew!" He smirked.

"No way! You had no idea. You were totally wrong! I stumped you. Admit it!"

"Never!" he shouted.

Several people turned to see what the ruckus was about.

Lucy laughed some more, grabbed his arm, and pulled him to hurry down the road.

Zinnie watched. Her heart swelled at the closeness they shared. She discovered that her lips turned up in a smile and her eyes stung.

Her heart squeezed. She had just spent the better part of an entire day learning how to pick the lock on their father's study. So she could steal something that was probably of great value to them.

"No, they won't even realize it's missing… whatever 'it' turns out to be," she whispered to herself.

Lela, whom Zinnie had forgotten was there, huffed a smoky breath out that stung Zinnie's eyes in a different way.

"*He's* handsome," a sly feminine voice spoke low into her ear.

Zinnie jumped and spun on her heels.

Jessamine stood in front of her with her arms folded and a smug expression on her face.

Zinnie pressed her hand against her chest to slow her heart.

"Your observation skills are as dismal as your appearance." She looked Zinnie up and down with a disappointed gaze. "Have you not been practicing like you should?" Jessamine raised her eyebrows and watched Zinnie fumble for a response. Her smugness turned to satisfaction.

"No. I mean, yes, of course I have. I was just… distracted." Zinnie knew she sounded desperate. She forced her mind and body to relax and prepare for whatever Jessamine wanted from her.

The woman never approached her in public. Although

the dark alley where they stood could hardly be considered public.

Jessamine stepped beside Zinnie and watched Atlas and Lucy disappear from sight.

"Like I said, he sure is handsome…" Jessamine's eyes looked greedy. "And your age, probably. And *look*, he has a sister. Isn't that sweet?" Her voice dripped with contempt.

Zinnie forced her breathing and face to remain calm and neutral. She couldn't let Jessamine know how much she had been startled by her sudden presence. And by the sinister words that ushered from her mouth. She had a sudden instinct to protect Atlas, even though she barely knew him.

Jessamine rested a firm hand on Zinnie's shoulder. "I think I know a way for you to get inside the house again…"

Zinnie's stomach dropped to her toes. She felt the blood drain from her face. She hoped her instincts in this situation were wrong, but they were usually accurate.

Jessamine tugged on one of Zinnie's blond curls. "I'll see you at home for supper. Then we can make plans. Don't dilly dally like you usually do."

The woman disappeared among the people and left Zinnie standing frozen to the spot.

Her mind raced. Had Jessamine followed her? What was she doing in this part of the city?

And what new idea did she have for Zinnie to retrieve the map that she mysteriously wanted? Zinnie didn't want to know.

Before Zinnie realized what she was doing, she beat a hasty retreat to the far wall on the far northern side of the city. Away from the palace. Away from Jessamine's shop, and the gate, and the market, and everything. Her heart pounded. Her feet slapped against the cobblestone street.

She dodged manticores, horse drawn carts, and crowds of people. She skidded around corners. By the time she reached the protective barrier she was out of breath, her hair was a frizzy mess, and she felt frantic.

She looked over her shoulder in both directions to make sure no one was watching her. Of course no one was. She was a short, wild girl on the outskirts of a corrupt city full of people that only cared about themselves.

She ducked behind a stable full of unsettled feathercorns pawing at the ground with their feathered hooves. It might have been her own demeanor that agitated them, or it might just be their nature. She didn't know and didn't care.

In the shadows right at the base of the wall she found what she had come for.

She dropped to her knees and shoved away the crates that she had carefully placed there months before to hide her secret.

A sink hole. The cliffs from beneath the city had crumbled in this spot. The ground and cobblestones beneath her feet had fallen far down to the rocky beach below.

She breathed in the salty air and squinted to see the beach far beneath. She daydreamed about escaping the city and combing the debris below for items of value that she could carry away and pawn for money. She would travel far from the City of Dorian to make her own way in the world. No more stealing. No more deception.

"I know it's just a dream, Lela," she said to her friend. "But it's better to dream about freedom than to succumb to the despair that threatens me in this place."

Lela blinked at Zinnie. She rubbed her feathers against Zinnie's chin and tugged on her curls.

"Thanks, Lela. You are a good friend."

Zinnie pulled herself from the ground and trudged through the city toward Jessamine's shop.

By the time Zinnie returned home, the sun had sunk below the wall that kept Zinnie prisoner high above the

Dorian Sea.

"I *told* you to be home for supper," Jessamine scolded.

"I know, I'm sorry. I just… needed to get some shells to grind into paint as part of the plan to break into the Forster's study. It's all very complicated…"

"Yes, yes." Jessamine waved her hand in the air to dismiss Zinnie's excuses. "Do not become long-winded. I trust you will accomplish the thing I have asked of you. And I know just how you will." She motioned for Zinnie to sit at the table in the kitchen.

"In one week, the new family- *Atlas's* family-" She gave Zinnie a pointed look, "is having a formal soiree. You will attend the party and use it as a way to obtain the item that I require. If the family suspects anything, just cozy up to the young man whom you so admire."

Zinnie blushed. She didn't "admire him." She simply found him… attractive. She was a young woman. She was allowed to find someone attractive, wasn't she?

Other questions popped into her head. What item did Jessamine want from them? It had to be a map.

How was she supposed to cozy up to Atlas? Would that really be a good enough distraction to be able to steal whatever it was that Jessamine wanted?

And what if he recognized her? What if his father found her familiar and realized she had been in their house before?

And what if Atlas ended up *actually* liking her? The last thing she wanted was to hurt him by faking affection for him. Even though she performed a lot of dishonest tasks for Jessamine, she had never manipulated someone's feelings before.

As if the woman read her thoughts, Jessamine said, "Don't worry, a boy from a wealthy family like that would never fall for a girl like yourself. Especially if he ever found out about what a deceitful person you are. Just get the job done. Is that clear?"

According to Jessamine, Zinnie would never be good enough for anyone to truly love her. Like her wishes for freedom from Jessamine and the City of Dorian, love was a dream that she should never expect to see fulfilled.

Zinnie kept a polite smile on her face but inwardly her stomach turned over. "Yes, ma'am." Her heart ached. Jessamine was right. No one would ever find her worthy of any sort of affection. She kept her face neutral. "May I go to bed now?"

Jessamine patted Zinnie's head in a condescending manner. "I do need you well rested if you are going to actually pull this off."

"Thank you." Zinnie stood to go.

Jessamine reached out and gripped Zinnie's wrist with one hand. The petite size of Jessamine's hand belied her strength. Her eyes pierced through Zinnie's as if she could read her thoughts. "Do *not* fail me, *Little Flower*."

Zinnie nodded and waited for Jessamine to release her grasp.

Her mistress held on just long enough to make Zinnie uncomfortable, then she released her.

Zinnie hurried to her room and shut the door tight. She leaned against it and breathed heavily.

"Oh, Lela," she moaned. "How am I supposed to do this?"

She had nightmares all night of pretending to fall in love with Atlas only to have him discover her secret, have her arrested, and thrown into the dungeon. Or worse, the prison tower on the far side of the palace.

The tower grew in height in the dream as she stood and stared up at it, until its pointed top reached into the clouds. There was no door. No way in or out. She would be trapped there. Alone. Forever.

She awoke in a cold sweat.

That would not be the way her life ended. She would decide her own fate. And she wouldn't let anyone, or any *map*, stop her.

Determined to keep her heart firmly protected from Atlas's stormy gaze, she made the arrangements for the upcoming formal soiree.

As usual, Jessamine left Zinnie to figure out the details for herself. And to provide herself with her own supplies by any means necessary. Well, any means besides money, of which Zinnie had none nor access to. She would have to trade for- or steal- anything she required.

Chapter 11

Zinnie knew how to get what she needed without the need to cheat, lie, or steal. Whenever she could, she employed this method, which would be perfect for acquiring the items for the party. Less guilt on her part, more satisfaction for those she interacted with. Everyone walked away a winner.

She started with something small, like a brooch or pirate coin, and made a mental list of anyone who may be interested in trading for it.

Once she traded slightly up, she would trade the next item for something bigger or better. Eventually she would have what she needed: a gown, gloves, shoes, ribbons, lace, and maybe a better pair of scissors. Hers were becoming dull. A fancy pair at the tailor had caught her eye before. But she knew in the end she would only procure what she needed and nothing more.

By the night of the party, she had added several more lengths of hair to her stash beneath her bed, mastered the unique lock she would need to crack, obtained all the necessities for her high-class disguise, and even gathered some brownie-made spark sticks to use as a distraction, just in case.

If Zinnie had ever felt like a fraud it was the night of the party.

She added layers of luxurious fabrics and opulent jewelry to her body within the walls of her dingy, back bedroom barely big enough to take three steps across. She pushed the condescending thoughts about not deserving to wear these items out of her mind. She shut down the guilt that threatened to plague her for possibly having to deceive a seemingly kind person like Atlas. She focused on the task of putting on the clothing.

"Lela, how do women dress like this every day?" She huffed as she tucked her cotton chemise into her matching bloomers.

She held up the body shaping corset lined with flying-whale bones and designed to shape her body into a more feminine figure.

"I mean, look at this! It's like a… trap, or something!" She sighed and wrapped the corset around her torso. "Do I even need this?"

She pulled the laces tight behind her. Fortunately, the flexibility that served her so well in her less-than-wholesome ventures also provided her with the means to tighten her own corset.

While her fingers conquered the strings, her stomach twisted in knots. Her mind played through her plan over and over again.

Arrive at the party. Slip away, pick the lock, steal the map.

She reminded herself that the fancy clothes would allow her to blend in.

Once the corset was secure, she ran her hands down her torso and looked in the mirror.

"Well, I can see now that it works." She tipped her head sideways and pulled at the top of the corset to try to better cover her bulging chest.

"This is ridiculous!" she said to herself this time. "Alright, what's next?"

She searched her lady-like knowledge for the information she needed. Her memory clicked and she added the short, shirt-like garment over the corset to protect the next layer of clothing, which turned out to be a narrow petticoat to cover the bloomers.

She added the bustle shaping-skirt next, which was simply a bag of cloth filled with horsehair tied around her waist.

"Why do women think this makes them look *good?*" Zinnie twisted to peer at her backside in the mirror. "I'll never understand high society."

She attempted to prepare herself for any number of scenarios.

If Gentleman Forster recognized her? *Play innocent.*

How about they called her out on her made-up family? *They just haven't met them yet.*

What if she got caught in part of the house she should not be in? *She got turned around trying to find fresh air.*

And if they didn't believe her story? *Cozy up to Atlas, like Jessamine suggested.*

The worst one of all: What if Atlas just… didn't *like* her?

For some reason that stung her heart in a way she had never experienced before. She had never given much thought to boys or romance or her future. She was, after all, just a deceitful nobody.

She continued to add layer after layer of clothing. More petticoats, the floor length skirt with a modest train, the matching bodice that came down to a point over her navel, and all the additional laces and ruffles that draped over the skirt in the front and the bustle at the back.

She let out a sigh while tying and placing the various garments over one another.

"What I wouldn't give to escape the city. Make my way across Tala." She glanced at Lela who watched her with interest.

The dragon let out a sigh, much like Zinnie's.

Zinnie chuckled. She furrowed her brow. "Do you think Jessamine would follow me if I managed to escape? Would she send one of her other employees to capture me and bring me back? She never says it, but I can see that my unique *talents* are very valuable to her. And she does comment on my remarkably youthful appearance."

She didn't expect Lela to respond. And the dragon just stared.

"It doesn't matter," she sighed again. "I just need to focus on tonight. I need to accomplish this thing for Jessamine, keep Atlas and his family safe. That's all that really matters right now."

When she had finished dressing, she turned to face Lela.

"Well?" She smoothed the front of the dress with her palms. "What do you think?"

Lela let out a breath of orange flames followed by a puff of smoke.

Zinnie tipped her head back and laughed out loud. "Nice, Lela."

She turned to look at her own reflection.

Having styled her hair before dressing, her outfit was nearly complete. She gasped when she saw her reflection. For all the seemingly unnecessary layers that filled out the shape of the look, Zinnie did not expect to see a woman standing where a simple girl had been only moments before.

The bodice hugged her waist, and the corset pressed her chest upward. The lace adornments she added covered her chest and shoulders enough to stay within fashion while still being modest enough for Zinnie's preferences. The skirt and layers of petticoats gave her bottom half a narrow bell shape that contradicted her non-existent hips and skinny legs. The low-heeled satin shoes on her feet did little to add to her height but did everything to make her look all grown up.

The abundance of curls pinned in a pile on top of her head, with wisps framing her face, ears, and neck made it so her dark lashes and full lips stood out. The layers were warm, but that added rosiness to her cheeks that was not normally present.

Tears stung Zinnie's eyes. If she didn't know better, she would have thought that a stranger stared back at her.

She wiped away the tears before they could fall. "Well, this is all a bit much."

She tried to brush away her emotions by talking to Lela about the other accessories spread across her bed. A low hat with feathers meant to be pinned to her hair. Wrist length white gloves for modesty, which seemed absurd since her arms and chest were bare! A lacy fan. That would be a necessity. She'd be lucky if she didn't pass out from overheating! And a small pouch that would dangle from her wrist.

"What do you think, Lela? Want to hop in and come with me?"

The dragon flapped her wings and flew herself back into her cage. She pulled the door shut with one of her taloned feet.

Zinnie laughed out loud again. "Alright, alright, I get the picture. How about I leave the cage open tonight if you promise to stay in my room?"

Lela pushed the door open and batted her long feathery eyelashes and Zinnie.

Zinnie took a deep breath and blew it out slowly. She looked at her reflection again. "Watch out, Atlas, here I come."

Whispers circled the open room at the mansion house where Atlas and his family lived.

"This was supposed to be soiree, not a ball!"

"Do they not know the difference between dancing and entertainment?"

"I was under the impression there would be appetizers and drinks."

The complaints came from men and women who resided in and around the palace.

Zinnie tuned out these voices, as well as others whispering about secrets and in judgement of one another.

She inwardly rolled her eyes. No one here behaved in a trustworthy manner, yet they all pretended to trust each other. They were all fools.

Zinnie avoided introductions at all costs, but when one was required, she claimed to be a friend of a cousin of a sister's aunt. The confusing statement shut most people up and she moved on before more questions could be asked.

She knew it would be difficult to gain Atlas's attention. It was his family's party after all, and everyone wanted to meet the new family. Mostly to determine their weaknesses and fears that could be preyed upon.

Zinnie wanted to tell them to leave this place and travel far across Tala and never look back. Maybe she would once she had the map.

Some of the whispers were correct, of course. A soiree should not have dancing. Whether they knew this and didn't care or were naïve about the difference didn't really matter. An orchestra played music from one end of the hall; and couples nervously danced with one another in a stiff manner down the center.

Fortunately, Zinnie had been trained in all the ways of ladylike behavior and knew these dances, as well as how to carry herself in high society. She used the fan to cool the sweat that wanted to bead on her forehead. The room was stuffy and the air thick.

A tall gentleman that Zinnie recognized from his dealings with Jessamine asked her to dance. She politely refused. She could not risk being recognized. Not yet anyway.

When another young man whom she did not recognize invited her onto the dance floor, she reluctantly agreed. She performed the dance perfectly, bored by the slow pace and forced conversation.

Just as the music ended, Atlas caught her eye. He was momentarily free from conversation. Now would be the perfect opportunity to try to draw an invitation from him for a turn around the dance floor.

She hurried through the sticky crowd to where he stood, and she brushed against him as she walked past. When she did so she dropped her fan and hesitated ever so slightly before continuing across the room.

"Miss," he called. "You dropped this."

His steel eyes locked onto her icy ones and his dimples appeared when he reached out to return her fan.

She rested her fingers delicately on her bare chest and gasped. "Oh my, thank you so much! I didn't realize I had even dropped it!"

She fluttered her eyelashes and gave him her most dazzling smile.

He blinked and nodded. "You're... you're welcome." His voice sounded tight.

She dipped into a slight curtsy and turned away from him as if to continue her path through the room.

"Wait!" He called after her again.

She returned to stand closer to him than she had before. The nearness made her blush. Fortunately, because of the stuffiness of the room, he probably wouldn't notice.

"May I have the pleasure of your hand for the next dance?" he asked. His voice cracked a little at the end of his sentence and he cleared his throat.

She suppressed a giggle and told her heart to calm down. This is exactly what she had planned. She couldn't become enamored by his handsome features and dreamy eyes.

Chapter 12

They stepped toward each other, away, joined hands in a half turn and back again. Atlas did not take his soft eyes off her face. He studied her hair, eyes, and, to Zinnie's surprise, her lips.

She pretended not to notice, and just continued to smile charmingly back at him.

When the dance was finished, neither had spoken a word.

"It's hot in here," Zinnie announced, probably a little too suddenly. She covered up her embarrassment with her fan.

"It is. Shall we step outside for a moment? The property came with an extensive garden in the courtyard." He motioned toward the back of the room.

"Oh, yes. Thank you!" She paused. "I don't think I even know your name!" She giggled and fanned her face.

He took her hand and tucked it into the crook of his arm to escort her to the garden.

"My name is Atlas. And you are?" He leaned close so she could hear him over the noise of the party.

"Zinnie. Nice to meet you."

"Nice to meet you too, Zinnia. That's a beautiful name, like the flower…"

She blushed. Again. "It would be," she teased. "If my name *was* Zinnia, like the flower. But it's just Zinnie. No 'a'." She fluttered her eyelashes and smiled to demonstrate she was not offended by his mistake.

"Of course. Well… Zinnie is a beautiful name, too. And it still reminds me of the flower…" He stumbled over his response.

She squeezed his arm and grinned at him.

He tripped over his feet because he couldn't keep his eyes off of her.

When they exited the building into the cool evening air, Zinnie breathed a sigh of relief.

Atlas laughed openly. "I couldn't agree more!" he announced.

Her plan was going even better than she had imagined. He had already invited her to be alone with him, which in any other place was probably not proper, but in the City of Dorian there were no such standards. They would stroll through the garden together. She would ask him about his father's business. His own hobbies. What books he liked to read, and hopefully lead the conversation to maps. She would flirt and ask to see them for herself, and he would readily agree. He was already smitten. This would not take long.

"So, Atlas," she started. She leaned a little closer to him, making sure her shoulder pressed against his arm. She held his arm a little tighter for good measure, too. "Where is your family originally from?"

She would have to guide the conversation carefully so as not to raise any suspicions that she already knew more about him than he could possibly know about her.

"We traveled nearly the entire length of Tala to arrive here. It took two whole weeks! But we were able to see so many amazing things. In fact, when we crossed the Graufast Mountains, I could have sworn I saw a griffin in the clouds. A real griffin!"

Zinnie beamed up at him. "That's so amazing!"

She opened her mouth task him another carefully crafted question, when an all too familiar voice called his name.

"Atlas!" His father's voice sounded muffled against the backdrop of sounds from the party. "Are you out here? You must return to the soiree and greet more guests." His voice did not sound unkind, but also carried the weight of a command, not a request.

Atlas sighed. "I'm sorry, Zinnie. I must do as Father says." He turned to face her in the moonlight. "Hopefully we'll see one another at another event or party sometime soon. Good night." He bowed slightly at the waist and jogged to return into the house to fulfill his hosting duties.

Zinnie stood there. Slack jawed. Speechless. What just happened? He abandoned her? Did she read him wrong? He seemed interested in her, hadn't he? Was he just being polite?

Her heart stung from the sudden rejection. Then she realized the real problem. She could not worm her way into the house without him. Should she use her explosives as a distraction? Draw the guests out of the party so she could slip inside?

She could barely move in this get up, though. But she must try.

With the other guests distracted by the unexpected

dancing, Zinnie returned to the interior of the house. She exited the dining room-turned-dance floor and stepped lightly down the hall. She would check the library across the entrance hall. A good number of the maps hung on the walls and rested in volumes on the numerous shelves.

Zinnie imagined the one Jessamine had described to her. It would be the length of her forearm and nearly as wide. The City of Dorian would feature on it, but other than that, she had mentioned only that there would be an "X" on it. Somewhere.

It wasn't a lot of information to go off of, but if she had the right amount of time, Zinnie was sure she would be able to locate it. Or at least one like it. Or maybe take home multiple maps that fit the description?

She pondered how to search the library as stealthily as she could in this restrictive clothing.

"Miss?" The familiar voice of the butler reached her ears. "The party is this way. I must ask you to remain either in the ballroom or the adjoining garden."

Zinnie raised her eyebrows at the use of the word "ballroom." This house had no such space, but the Forster's didn't seem to worry about that detail.

"Oh! Of course, I do apologize." She reverted to the excuse she had prepared. "I got turned around looking for the garden." She gave the butler her most dazzling smile, kept her posture straight, and exuded all the confidence in the world.

The man dipped his head and returned a friendly smile. He helped shuffle her back into the stifling party.

The thought of retreating to the garden and letting loose her spark sticks crossed her mind, but the panic that could ensue might not work in her favor.

She tucked herself in the corner and waited for another moment to sneak into the library.

While she waited her eyes scanned the room. Some of the

guests appeared to have a great time at the party, while others hid behind fans and feathers with keen eyes keeping track of their own targets. Everyone played some kind of game. Hopefully no one else had designs for Jessamine's map. If someone else got to it first, Zinnie would be in very hot water.

Her eyes landed on Atlas again. He greeted the guests beside his parents. His warm smile and easy laughter endeared him to nearly everyone who crossed through the party.

Zinnie found herself smiling in his direction, too. Imagined what he might be saying to the people. Pretending that she stood with her hand in the crook of his arm.

His eyes darted around the room from time to time, as if he might be looking for someone. Perhaps Zinnie?

"Nonsense," she whispered to herself. "There are plenty of more fashionable young women in the room than me."

But her heart reminded her of the way he held her gaze earlier. How his touch and closeness had left her feeling flustered. No one would notice, of course, since she hid it well. But it had happened, she had to admit to herself.

"*Do your job, Zinnie*," she scolded. "Attract his attention. Get him to invite you into the library. Do *something!*"

She pushed her way through the crowd, but before she could reach the other side of the room, Atlas was dancing with another of the women from the city. Zinnie's heart dropped. He gave her the same warm smile he had given to Zinnie. And to everyone else in the room.

Jessamine told you it wasn't a risk that he would fall for you. You just need to be more forward.

But after the next dance, his father pulled him away again to speak with one of the city leaders. Zinnie shrunk away. She couldn't be seen here by that man. It would not end well for either her or Jessamine.

She ducked out of sight to wait for another chance. But between the introductions Atlas's father made and the dances he had to participate in, the moment never came.

Zinnie left the home at the end of the evening with sore feet and a troubled mind. She had failed to achieve her objective for the very first time in years. She hadn't had that much bad luck since she was a young girl.

"Oh, Lela." She spoke as if her dragon friend could hear her from so far away. "Mistress Jessamine is going to be furious…"

"What do you *mean* you didn't retrieve the map? That was the whole reason I allowed you to go to the soiree at all! I knew you were a foolish girl, but I did not expect you to return with nothing!"

Jessamine pinched her lips and rubbed her forehead. Her scowl deepened. She breathed in deep and let it out slowly. "I am trying not to be angry with you, but you are making it difficult for me. I asked you to do this *one thing* for me."

Zinnie wanted to argue *so badly*. 'This one thing?' 'Allow her to go to the party?' As if she had a choice in the matter. And she had to do all the preparations by herself! Mistress Jessamine practically set her up for failure.

While Zinnie bit her tongue, Jessamine murmured to herself about finding another way to retrieve the map. She glared at Zinnie; the word "useless" on her breath.

Zinnie's heart seized. Her feelings hurt. She had only done everything Jessamine had ever asked, for good and bad, and now the woman referred to her as useless and foolish?

"You will be punished for this failure. An entire day locked in your room. No food. Your punishment begins now. Go." Jessamine turned her back to Zinnie.

Zinnie's heart cracked. *Now* Jessamine acted like a parent? Punishing her for something completely out of her control?

This is where most teenagers would argue. Demand their

side of the story be heard. But Zinnie knew better than to try. Jessamine didn't seem to have a heart at all.

Zinnie simply stated her usual, "Yes, ma'am," and turned to leave the kitchen.

Jessamine continued to calculate how to acquire the map she wanted in a timely manner. As if she had a deadline.

Zinnie shuddered at the thought. She stepped into her room and closed the door.

Would Jessamine really lock it behind her? The click of the handle answered that question.

"As if a lock like *that* could even keep me inside…" she grumbled to herself.

But she knew that Jessamine knew the truth. Zinnie would not argue. She would not try to leave the room. She would be obedient, as always.

The oppression wrapped around Zinnie. She wanted to scream! To throw something. Maybe have a tantrum like Jessamine had only a few days ago! Why did Zinnie have to be perfect all the time? It wasn't fair.

Lela soared across the room and hovered in front of Zinnie until the girl cupped her hands for a landing place. She cooed at Zinnie and fluffed her feathers.

"I don't know exactly what you're trying to say to me, Lela, but I appreciate the sentiment all the same. Thank you."

She lowered herself stiffly on the bed. The corset prevented her from slouching, and also from taking a very deep breath in the seated position.

"I was such a fool to think I could pull this off. I'm nothing but a simple girl in a fancy dress. I don't deserve someone like Atlas, anyway."

She sucked in a breath. Was she more upset about not retrieving the map and incurring her mistress's anger, or because she hadn't been able to entice Atlas?

She fell backwards on the bed and groaned.

Chapter 13

A day spent cooped up in her room was possibly one of the worst punishments Zinnie could imagine. She paced like a caged animal.

Zinnie spent time studying the few books on her shelf, practicing picking the collection of locks she kept in the case beneath the bed, expertly braiding her hair into an array of intricate designs, and even performing sleight of hand card tricks for Lela. She even resorted to playing hide and seek with the dragon. But since the room was so small the game didn't last long.

By the end of the day boredom threatened Zinnie's sanity. She stroked the dragon's silky feathers for comfort.

Lela primped and spun in the air before landing on the bed beside Zinnie again.

Zinnie sighed. "What will we do

once we figure out a way to escape? I want to climb to the top of a mountain! See a pegasus… or maybe ride one!" She sat up and looked at Lela with wide eyes. "Do you think I could ride one?"

Lela shook her head.

Zinnie fell backwards again. "How about a dragon, then? I'm sure *you* could put in a good word for me, right?"

Lela squeaked.

"I'll take that as a yes!"

By the time Zinnie woke up the following morning, Mistress Jessamine had already unlocked her bedroom door.

Zinnie was free- though not really. Freedom from her locked room felt good, but it wasn't the freedom she truly desired.

She sighed, hurried to cut her hair, get dressed, and joined Jessamine in the kitchen for breakfast.

She kept her head down and avoided eye contact. She slid into her seat and whispered, "Good morning, Mistress Jessamine."

Her mistress chewed her measly porridge slowly. Zinnie could feel the woman's gaze on her.

"I…" She swallowed the lump of… fear? Shame? Both? That lodged in her throat. "I'm sorry about the… party."

Jessamine's metal spoon clanked onto the tabletop when she set it down a little harder than necessary. "Yes, well." The woman dabbed her face with her dingy cloth napkin. Her chair legs scraped on the uneven floor. "I have made other… arrangements… to acquire the item that I need from that family."

She turned on her heel and marched the three steps to the opposite wall, setting her dishes down with a clatter. "Get these cleaned up and find me in my shop. I will you give you your tasks for the day."

Zinnie did as she was told, as usual, and padded into the

shop.

"I really am sorry about the party. I did try. Atlas was called away by his father to greet guests…"

Jessamine held up her hand for Zinnie to stop talking.

Zinnie felt completely responsible for her failure. She should have tried harder. She should have been more forward with Atlas. Her foolishness and carelessness had gotten the best of her, just like Jessamine said.

"What's done is done. I don't need to hear your pathetic excuses. However, I *must* have the map. I do not wish to wait for it. I have other means to retrieve it, and I will use them."

What *other means* would the woman use to get the map? Images flashed through Zinnie's mind. Jessamine's henchmen breaking into the home? Someone employing one of her strange potions to disable the family so Jessamine could just walk in and take the map? Something else? The woman kept many secrets from Zinnie.

Would her *other means* put Atlas or his family in harm's way?

"Please, Mistress." Zinnie checked her voice. She couldn't sound too invested in Atlas or the map. She slowed her speech. "I know I can figure out a way. I can win him over, maybe even convince him to *give* me the map! Then you wouldn't run any risks of being accused…"

Jessamine gave her a sharp look.

Zinnie pinched her lips closed.

A calculating expression crossed Jessamine's face. She opened her mouth to speak to Zinnie, but the door to the shop burst open. A harried looking, dirty clothed man barged into the room.

"Ma'am, you are needed in the dungeons, at once!" He ran out the door the way he had come.

The dungeons? Why was Jessamine needed in the dungeons? The thought of what she could possibly be doing down there startled Zinnie. She had always known that Jessamine was a little dangerous, but only in the way that she could destroy someone's livelihood. She couldn't imagine the woman would do anything to physically harm someone. Would she?

Jessamine's nostrils flared and she snapped her eyes back to Zinnie. "Stay here. I will return shortly."

Without a backwards glance she left the shop faster than Zinnie had ever witnessed before. Normally her movements were carefully calculated. But Jessamine acted frantic.

Zinnie did as she was told and paced back and forth near the front windows. They were too dark and dusty to see anything other than silhouettes of passersby, but she anxiously awaited her mistress's return.

Worry ate away at Zinnie's insides. She didn't know that this whole venture could potentially put Atlas at risk like this. How could she protect them if she had no idea what her mistress was up to?

To keep her mind off of her spiraling thoughts, Zinnie focused on tidying up the shop.

The bottles of dried herbs that lined one narrow shelf needed straightening. The labeled jars of potions and poisons sat adjacent. Zinnie didn't like touching those. Not knowing exactly what was inside made her nervous. She left them alone.

She ran her fingers along the spines of disorganized books as she walked past. The sensation of the various textures and sizes tickled her fingertips.

She restacked the crates in one corner, ignoring the fact that she didn't really know, and didn't really want to know, exactly what they contained.

The spider that dangled from its web in one corner watched her with its oversized eyes. She let it be. It hadn't threatened her and if anything, it kept the other, creepier bugs to a minimum.

A dust bunny poked its head out from beneath one of the trunks filled with pawned, out-of-season clothing. It pinned its beady eyes on her, wiggled its nose, and retreated out of sight again.

Zinnie passed by the window. When would Jessamine return?

Long after Zinnie's usual lunch hour Jessamine finally returned. The woman looked unsettled, disheveled. And angry.

Zinnie knew better than to ask any questions or say anything to her. At all. About anything.

The woman marched past Zinnie toward the back of the shop.

Without making eye contact Jessamine grumbled, "You have until the next full moon. Take care of it or things will *not* end well for Atlas and his family. I have other things I need to focus on for now."

"Yes, mistress," Zinnie answered softly.

Her heart skipped a beat. This would be her only chance to accomplish her task and hopefully prevent Jessamine from harming the Forster's.

Jessamine slammed her own bedroom suite door. The sounds of things being banged around shook the walls. An earthen container crashed onto the floor.

Zinnie flinched. A cold sweat ran down her back. She'd never seen Jessamine so angry. Threatening. Uncaring. Her usual mask of civility had disappeared completely.

Who was this woman she had been living with for almost her entire life? And how dangerous was she?

Zinnie continued to stare in the direction Jessamine had gone.

"I will figure this out. I will protect Atlas's family."

Another clang came from Jessamine's rooms.

Zinnie flinched.

A new sense of urgency ran through her veins. Maybe it was time for Zinnie to really figure out how to leave the City of Dorian.

Chapter 14

The new, expensive-looking outfit only cost Zinnie the packet of golden dorma flower pollen. She knew where to acquire more, so it was a small price for daytime clothing that would allow her to blend in with more polite society than her usual dealings.

Zinnie turned side to side to admire her handiwork. Her fresh shoulder length curls pinned into a classy updo on the back of her head gave her the appearance of youthful maturity.

"At least this clothing is a little easier to move around in," Zinnie said to Lela while examining her reflection. "No skirt supports or corsets today. And with so many less layers I'll be able to breathe in the afternoon sun."

The lighter-weight skirt gathered at her waist and flared to her toes. The neckline- higher than the party dress but lower than a typical work dress- and elbow-length lace sleeves let cool air through. The pastel blue fabric matched her eyes.

She decided against the usual bonnet or hat and pinned a fresh daisy blossom in the hair over her ear, instead.

"Good enough to look decent but comfortable enough to get things done, if necessary. You ready, Lela?"

With the dragon in place behind her shoulder length loose curls, Zinnie made her way across town, toward the city library.

She perused row upon row of towering shelves filled with more books than a person could read in an entire lifetime. The library's convenient location near the palace offered at least a somewhat good chance of spotting Atlas. Plus, Zinnie had it on good authority- gossip from the house maids- that Atlas enjoyed searching for new volumes to study.

Her peripheral vision and keen ears stayed alert for any signs of Atlas.

Would he spend time at the library that day? What if he didn't? His family did have an extensive collection of their own. Maybe the housemaids were mistaken, and he liked to spend time perusing his own collection at home for new volumes to study

While she fretted over whether she would see Atlas at all, she also listened for any information that could prove useful for getting back onto Jessamine's good side. The comments about the full moon, and rumors of violent animal behavior, combined with the woman's alarming behavior lately, left a cloud of dread over Zinnie. Should Zinnie fear for her *own* safety, in addition to Atlas and his family?

She *had* to succeed today. She only had three weeks left until the next full moon. Then she could begin to think about her own escape.

That statement from Jessamine about the full moon being the deadline had bothered Zinnie. She allowed her focus to wane. The next full moon? Why so specific? Zinnie had heard things before about creatures that turned violent on the night of the full moon. Did that have anything to do with

Jessamine's plan to get the map for herself?

Zinnie's palms moistened. She turned the pages in the book she was holding, but her eyes did not register the words.

An alluring male voice spoke right into Zinnie's ear from behind. "What would a young lady like yourself need to know about dwarf warfare?"

She jumped and snapped the book shut.

The voice laughed out loud.

Zinnie turned her surprised face toward the enchanting sound.

She pressed her hand against her chest. "Atlas! You startled me!"

Rarely had anyone been able to sneak up on her like that before. She was always the one doing the sneaking!

The way his eyes crinkled at the corners and his lips pulled into a wide, relaxed smile didn't do anything to help slow her racing heart.

She felt her cheeks flush. She told herself she was just embarrassed at having been the victim for once.

"Zinnie, it is good to see you!" Atlas's voice was low and warm.

She dipped her head. "And you." She remembered her ladylike manners in such a situation.

She carefully replaced the book on the shelf and fully turned to face Atlas. Her heart continued to thump against her ribcage.

"What brings you here? I would imagine your home has quiet the collection of books?" Zinnie remembered that she was supposed to not actually *know* that information. Hopefully he wouldn't notice her slip up.

He nodded. "It does. But it doesn't have quite the collection of *people*." His grin, impossibly, widened.

She giggled, then forced herself to calm down.

"I am glad I bumped into you again!" Atlas continued. "I am sorry I had to leave you so abruptly at the party before. My father insisted I greet as many guests as possible." Atlas shrugged. "I looked for you again, but you seemed to have disappeared."

She nodded. "Yes, I got lost in the crowd, I suppose."

She hadn't actually left, but he had been so wrapped up in talking to all the other people that he must not have noticed her. Again, she was just a nobody in a fancy dress.

She must not have done a very good job at keeping her polite mask on, because Atlas lowered his eyebrows and bent closer.

"Are you alright? Is anything the matter?" His hand reached out as if to touch her arm, but thought better of it and retreated.

She forced her face to relax into a comfortable smile once again. "Yes, of course. Just… distracted." At least *that* wasn't a lie. Those eyes…

As if on cue, Lela poked her head out from beneath Zinnie's blonde locks.

"Oh!" Atlas startled.

Zinnie smiled sweetly at him. "Atlas, meet Lela."

The feathered dragon shimmied down Zinnie's arm and rested in her palm. She wrapped her tail around Zinnie's wrist.

"A hummingbird dragon!" Atlas stepped closer to get a better look. "May I?" He raised his eyebrows at Zinnie and brought his hand closer to Lela.

Zinnie giggled. "Of course. She's quite friendly."

Atlas rubbed the top of Lela's head with one finger. His smile widened. "She's perfect," he announced.

Satisfied by the adoring attention, Lela made a sound like a purr. She flapped her wings and lifted herself to Zinnie's shoulder again.

Zinnie leaned toward Atlas and spoke in a whisper. "I'm

not really supposed to have her in here…"

"I see. Well, it was nice meeting you, Lela."

The dragon cooed at him, then disappeared beneath Zinnie's hair again.

"Does she accompany you all the time?"

If Zinnie were to answer honestly, it would be, "No". She frequently left the dragon home when she went on overnight jobs for Jessamine.

Hummingbird dragons were not nocturnal creatures and Lela preferred staying home for the late night and early morning activities.

"Most of the time," she answered instead. "One of the benefits of thick hair." She grinned at Atlas.

"May I walk with you while you peruse?" He gestured at the rows of books.

She really wanted to spend all afternoon in the library with him. Nothing sounded more dreamlike.

But the plan for that day was *not* to get the map. Or even enter his home. Today was just to get him to notice her. To want to spend more time with her. This would have to be a little bit longer of a con than a quick score.

By playing hard to get, it should make him desire her company even more.

At least, that's what she *hoped* would happen. She had no idea if he already had a woman he called upon, though that seemed unlikely since he had just recently arrived in the city.

She decided to stick with her original plan. "I'm sorry." She shook her head and gave him an apologetic look. "I must be on my way."

"Well, Zinnie-not-ZinniA. I do hope to see you again sometime. Perhaps someplace where we don't have to be so quiet." He grinned and tipped his head in her direction. "And you, too, Lela," he whispered near Zinnie's ear.

His closeness nearly disrupted her resolve. She hesitated.

She really didn't want to leave.

But the commitment to the con, and Jessamine's ominous deadline, pulled her away from him.

She peeked over her shoulder at him and was pleasantly surprised to find him still watching her. She told herself the giddy feeling came because the act was working. It didn't have anything to do with his handsome face and perfect manners. Nope. Not at all.

Zinnie expertly managed to "bump" into him again the following day at the market.

Lela had been stationed outside his home to watch him and see which way he was going. When she brought the message back to Zinnie, which she deciphered from the swoops of the dragon's flight path, Zinnie hurried out the door in her fancier clothing to "do her daily errands."

Jessamine's harsh reminder the night before repeated in her head. "Another day has passed. I hope you do not fail again. I would hate to see the unfortunate results."

The words hung over her when she cut her hair before bed and added the new locks to her hidden case. The words sat heavy on her shoulder while she tossed and turned all night, her imagination running away with her. And they squeezed her chest like a corset when she dressed that morning.

Today's goal would be to spend more time with him and leave him wanting to see her again. Maybe she'd even procure an invitation to see him again soon. In a few days she'd be back in his home, could easily use Lela as a distraction to discover where the specific map was in the home. Knowing where the item was located would allow her to proceed with a middle of the night theft. The job would be complete by the end of the week.

With the sun rapidly ascending toward late morning, Zinnie hurried to the market. She spotted the head of messy black hair and managed to nudge him from behind. She made it look like a total accident, and even hollered in surprise to find it was Atlas that had made her drop her basket of fresh vegetables she had purchased for her non-existent family's supper.

Atlas, of course, helped her pick them up.

When their hands brushed against one another a tingle lingered on Zinnie's hand. Her forget-me-not eyes jumped to his handsome face. Had he felt it too?

He didn't react at all.

Instead, he helped her stand and said, "I am purchasing supplies for a picnic outside the city with my sister. Have you been to the poppy meadow beyond the gates? It looks like something from a theater costume, doesn't it? When we traveled past it on our way in, Lucy insisted she wanted to lunch there as soon as possible." He paused. "Would you care to join us?"

Chapter 15

She couldn't believe it! An invitation to picnic with them? It was the perfect way to cozy up to him. This worked perfectly for her plan!

"Unfortunately," she did not have to simulate her disappointment, "I cannot leave the city. Today!" She hurried to add. "I cannot leave the city *today*."

Atlas's face fell. "Oh, it would have been so wonderful to have you join us."

She shook her head. "Besides that," she waved her hand, "you don't want to picnic in that meadow. Have you ever heard of poppy pixies?"

Atlas's eyes widened. "Poppy pixies? No!"

Zinnie snuck her hand around his arm and led him as she continued to walk up the rows of the market. She told him about the pixies while they both shopped for the items they had come for.

"The pixies born from poppy blossoms stay in their field their entire life. They wear robes the color of night with hoods that shade their faces from the sun. They're known to swarm anyone who steps foot in their home field. They have a vendetta against meadow animals and can take out even the fiercest badger or even an entire drove of thistlehares."

"But don't thistlehares have deadly antlers?" Atlas questioned.

Zinnie nodded. "The pixies develop their own weapons to fight off whatever animals try to come and eat their blossoms. Let's just say, they tend to go for the eyes."

Atlas cringed. "Ouch…"

"Yeah. You'd be much better off picnicking in your own garden, I assure you."

"Are there not pixies of that nature that reside here? In the city?" He looked around as if he might catch sight of one.

"No. There's… something about this place that repels the little fiends."

She had no real experience with the creatures herself but had heard horror stories from others about the variety of pixies and the trouble they could cause. "But there are plenty of other beings here. We certainly aren't lacking with the strange variety, even with a lack of pixies."

They walked along the city streets back towards Atlas's home. He carried her basket of totally unneeded vegetables- unbeknownst to him, of course- along with his own canvas sack of produce and cured meats.

"I've heard rumors there are pixies with healing magic?" Atlas quizzed Zinnie about her knowledge of the wonder to be found in the world.

"I don't know about that," she answered. "But there are stories of Forest People with healing abilities."

"Have you ever met one? A Forest Person?"

"No, have you?" He was more likely to since he had traveled so far, and she had never left the city.

"No. At least, not that I know of." He shrugged. "What

sorts of beings inhabit this place? Are there more like Lela around?"

Zinnie told Atlas about freeing Lela from the palace menagerie.

Atlas frowned. "I hate that some humans think they are better than all other creatures."

Zinnie pointed out many of the creatures and people they saw while they strolled along at a leisurely pace.

He had seen a few others on his own, including the gargoyles that sprang to life whenever someone tried to enter the palace gates.

"What about all the little flying things around? There seems to be no end to their variety."

Zinnie nodded. "With only one way in or out by land, and no natural water sources, we tend to harbor mostly flying animals. And there's probably way more variety than just what you've seen. Especially if you go out and about at night!"

The conversation paused as they both realized where they were.

"Well, this is where we part ways, I suppose." Zinnie stopped in front of Atlas's home and folded her hands in front of her.

Atlas turned to face her. His warm smile melted her insides. He shook the bag. "I have enough food for three…"

She raised her eyebrows. Was he still inviting her to a picnic with him and his sister? At their home?

She couldn't believe her good fortune. This would further her plan by an entire day, maybe two!

A prick of guilt stabbed her heart.

She shoved it aside and reminded herself to focus on the job at hand.

She smiled up at him and nodded. "I would very much enjoy that! Thank you." She gestured at her own basket hanging off his arm. "And please, feel free to use those as my contribution."

Her previous two experiences in the home had been extreme examples: slipping in through the servants' entrance the first time; and joining crowds of people for a party the second.

She delighted in the feel of normalcy that the house had that day with just Atlas.

The now-decorated entry hall had a round table for calling cards near the door, a bench with hooks for guests' overcoats, hats, and gloves, and a potted magnolia tree in one corner showing off its bright green leaves.

The aromas wafting from the kitchen made Zinnie's mouth water. The sounds of servants moving about the house filled the space with just enough background noise for it to not be deafeningly quiet or overly loud.

Atlas continued forward while Zinnie absorbed the opulent surroundings, rich fabrics, and deep colors of the home. Atlas kept talking to her, his voice echoing around the room.

She pulled herself together. She was supposed to be figuring out the location of the desired map, not gawking at the surroundings that should be familiar to another member of high society.

She hurried to catch up to Atlas.

"Lucy!" Atlas called up the curved staircase as he passed by. "I'll be in the back garden!" He didn't wait for his sister to respond or appear, just continued through the house toward the back. He pointed out the rooms as he went.

Some she had seen already at the party or when she had worked there for a day, others were new, though not important for Zinnie's mission.

She had to continuously remind herself that she was there to get the map. Or to get Atlas to give her the map. Not to make friends.

Still, the most convincing con was one that had a seed of truth to it.

"The house is so tidy!" Zinnie mentioned as she passed a narrow table in the hallway decorated with a small globe and a mariner's compass. "Do you have brownies to help keep house?" She kept up the pretense that she had only been here the one time at the party.

Atlas laughed over his shoulder. "Brownies? No! Of course not. They only live on farms and in the woods." He stopped short. "Wait. They *do* only live on farms or in the woods, right?" His eyes widened.

She smirked at him and pinched his arm. "Sure, if that helps you sleep at night…"

Zinnie brushed past him and continued forward. She didn't know exactly where she was going, but the garden at the back of the house was pretty self-explanatory. It was likely the one she had enjoyed with Atlas the night of the party, if only briefly.

It was Atlas's turn to catch up to Zinnie. He walked beside her, their shoulders brushing one another with every other step. "Are you telling me that brownies live in places like this, too?" He looked at the walls as if seeing them for the first time. "How do you know if you have brownies in your house?"

Zinnie's sparkling laugh filled the hallway. "You'd know, trust me." She nudged him. "I was mostly teasing. They do live in any number of places, but if you didn't bring some with you, then I doubt there are any here."

Atlas's shoulders relaxed.

"Wait, are you scared of brownies or something?" She grinned sideways at him.

"What? No! Well, I mean, I have heard stories of them tying your toes together while you sleep and such…"

"I think you'll be safe…"

Before Zinnie could finish teasing Atlas about the danger level of miniature men, another feminine voice echoed down the hall along with the sound of hurried footsteps behind them.

"Atlas! You're home!"

Zinnie turned around to greet Atlas's sister for the first time. She had seen her at the party but hadn't had the courage to speak with her. Especially since she thought she'd never see the family again after that night. But now it would make sense to get on Lucy's good side, as well as Atlas's.

She gave Lucy a warm smile. "Hello, I'm Zinnie." She dipped into a slight curtsy. "And this is Lela."

The dragon fluttered into the air, her wings a blur. She circled Lucy a few times and they hovered in front of the younger girl's face.

Lucy copied Zinnie's movement and beamed at Lela. "I'm Lucy. Nice to meet you." She stretched her hand toward Lela.

The hummingbird dragon alighted on her palm.

Lucy giggled. "It tickles!" Her face radiated her excitement. "You're Atlas's new friend, right Zinnie? He's told me a little bit about you."

Zinnie snapped her eyes onto Atlas's face. He had spoken to Lucy about her? What had he said? Her cheeks flushed, and Atlas gave her a mock guilty look and shrugged.

Lucy laughed. "Don't worry, not a lot. Just a few things. You have made quite the impression on him, though. He doesn't actually have any friends. Besides, me of course!"

"Hey!" Atlas scolded.

Lucy shrugged. "Its true." She leaned toward Zinnie with a look of mischief in her eyes. "We're only a year apart from each other in age. We're practically twins. I'm his only friend."

Atlas rolled his eyes. "*Practically twins*," he murmured. "We're more than a year apart, Lucy. Almost two, in fact.

And I do have friends…"

"Not here," Lucy countered.

Atlas began to disagree again, but Lucy interrupted him. "I'm starved. Let's go eat. You said we're going to the garden? Why not the poppy field?"

"I'll let Zinnie explain, come on." Atlas sighed and led the girls to the garden behind the house.

Chapter 16

Zinnie helped herself to the array of cured meats, hard cheese cubes, crisp crackers, dark olives, young broccoli stems, fingerling carrots, and grape-sized tomatoes. Her taste buds danced at the variety of textures and flavors compared to the bland, barely nutritious food she ate at Mistress Jessamine's table day in and day out. She had eaten each of these things before, of course, sometimes purchasing them herself, or trading a vendor for something of value. But she had never eaten an entire meal like this.

She hid her delight well, offering polite "thank you's" and compliments here and there instead of gushing about the quality and flavor of the food like she wanted to.

"Tell me about your family," Zinnie inquired between bites of the decadent morsels.

Atlas nodded to Lucy. "Go ahead," he encouraged.

Lucy's cheeks reddened. She shook her head shyly and gave him a pleading look.

He patted her hand, nodded, and returned his gaze to Zinnie. "We traveled from all the way across Tala."

Lucy nodded beside him. Zinnie nodded, too. She already knew this. She waited for him to say more.

"Our father is in the cartography business," Atlas said.

"Oh, he creates maps, then? Is he a Mapmaker?" She quizzed him about whether he had a magical compulsion for maps, or he just had skill as an artist and put his talent to use to create art in the form of maps.

At the mention of a Mapmaker, Lucy joined the conversation. "He *wishes* he was a Mapmaker!" She looked at Atlas with mischief.

Atlas nodded. "Yes, I suppose he does. But he does not have the gift of which you speak."

"He said he met one once though! A really long time ago." Lucy added before popping another black olive into her mouth.

"They are very rare, from what I understand," Zinnie agreed.

"He does have a knack for knowing where to find good maps, though. Not hidden ones, or anything, but more like an understanding of what kind of person might harbor a valuable map. He's managed to procure some very unique ones over time."

"Yes, and that's why we came here, isn't it?" Lucy chimed.

Atlas glanced her way, then back at Zinnie. He looked troubled.

"I won't say anything, if it's supposed to be a secret," Zinnie hurried.

Atlas's shoulders relaxed.

"Sorry," Lucy frowned. "It's just such a normal part of

our lives that I forgot that we aren't really supposed to talk about it here that much."

"Father has only announced that he is here to serve the city council, but he hasn't been forthright in the service he is to provide them."

Zinnie waited for one of them to say more. She wanted to ask, but didn't want to seem too eager, either. Why wouldn't their father want others to know about his knowledge and extensive collection? Why should it be kept secret?

A pit grew in Zinnie's stomach. This must have something to do with Jessamine. Was she in on the reason the council wanted their father to come? Or was she the reason his presence was supposed to remain a secret?

"I believe we can trust you." Lucy gave Atlas a pleading look. "Go on, Atlas, you can tell her."

Zinnie wanted to tell them not to trust her. She knew that any information they divulged she would have to share with Jessamine. She wanted to stand up, run away, and let them keep their secrets.

But Jessamine's sinister warning about the full moon came into Zinnie's mind. She bit her tongue and allowed them to continue sharing their family secrets.

"Father is more than just a map connoisseur. He has deep knowledge of many of the maps that are printed and formed. The city leaders sent word out that they were looking for a renowned map collector to come who had their own collection and extensive knowledge of map bibliographies, and so on."

"Map bibliographies?" Zinnie looked back and forth between the siblings.

"Yes. Who made a certain map, what is it for, that sort of thing."

"And why they made it, too," Lucy added.

The mood grew awkward as Zinnie tried to think of something to say. She didn't want to pry, mostly because that would seem strange, but she needed to cultivate this conversation. See if they would divulge any other secrets about what kind of maps the leaders want, or what they might be seeking from these maps.

"Let me get this straight," she said in a serious tone.

Atlas lowered his eyebrows and squinted at her.

"Your father collects maps. Studies them. Tracks them down better than most people?" She drew her eyebrows together as if she was testing the legitimacy of their claims.

"Yes," Atlas said in a firm voice. He leaned away from her and straightened his back.

"And when he found out he had a son, he decided to call you 'Atlas'?"

Lucy threw her head back and laughed out loud. The peels of laughter bounced around the garden.

Atlas froze, then melted into a smile once again. He chuckled in a self-deprecating way. "Yes, my father- the map collector- named his one and only son Atlas."

Zinnie shook her head. "That is very unfortunate, isn't it? Unless you plan on going into the family business, then it could be quite fortuitous!"

Atlas shook his head and chuckled again. "Maps aren't really my thing…"

Zinnie patted his arm. "That's probably for the best."

She allowed her hand to linger on his arm just a little bit longer than necessary. The heat that seeped up her own hand and into her arm from the touch surprised her, but she forced herself to remain calm and give him a lovely smile.

She pulled back and broke a chunk of cheese off the wheel. "At least *you* received a normal name, Lucy."

At this, Lucy laughed out loud again. "Not quite. You see, Lucy means light, and Father says that in order to study maps you need a good strong light to help you see." She shrugged.

"It's less obvious but very much just as intentional."

"And your mother didn't have any objections?" Zinnie looked back and forth between her two new friends.

"Mother and Father are so in love, they rarely object to anything the other does. It's quite romantic." Lucy sighed and a dreamy expression crossed her face. "I hope to find a love like that someday."

Zinnie wanted to tell her that she would find no such thing in this city, but she didn't want to spoil the girl's dreams.

Silence hung in the air for a few beats. Zinnie opened her mouth to ask another question to continue the topic of maps.

The door that they had emerged from opened before she could form her thoughts into a question.

"Atlas! There you are." The sibling's father burst through the door. "I need your help, son. I am in a hurry." He motioned for Atlas to follow him at once.

"Yes, Father. Is everything alright?" The younger version of the man in the doorway stood abruptly and gave Lucy a worried look.

"Yes, yes." Their father waved away his question. "I have an important meeting and I must carry a dozen maps with me. I don't trust the servants to be as careful with them as I know you will be. Don't delay... Oh! I see you have company..."

Zinnie ducked her head and allowed her blonde locks to hide her face as she pretended to pick up a morsel of food that she dropped. She peeked at their father through the curtain of curls.

Would he recognize her as the maid he nearly barreled into that first day? What would he do if he did?

But he was too distracted at the moment and didn't even wait for his children to introduce their guest. "Come along, Atlas." He rushed back through the door.

"I am so sorry, Zinnie. This shouldn't take long. I'll be back soon, I promise!" Atlas followed his father and left Zinnie on the ground with only Lucy for company.

It was like the world didn't want her to have the chance to find out what she needed to know. Every time she felt like she was getting close, Atlas's father pulled him away from her.

She refrained from huffing out a sigh. She wanted to get this over with before time ran out. Before Jessamine became impatient and went forward with whatever other plan she had for obtaining the map she wanted. Zinnie couldn't delay.

But she also couldn't risk Atlas's father recognizing her. And she didn't know how to explain her odd behavior when the man had appeared. She had been open and friendly with the siblings. How could she explain her uncomfortableness in the presence of their parent?

Her mind raced and she avoided eye contact with Lucy. If Gentleman Forster took the maps to the palace, then it wouldn't matter if Atlas returned to show Zinnie around. She wouldn't be able to scope out the map's location. She would not be able to return that night to acquire it. She'd have to figure out a way to be invited back another time. It would have to be soon. She couldn't waste time on this.

You have time, she reminded herself. *Today was a stroke of luck. Just keep the plan going. It will all be fine…*

"Should we clean this up?" Lucy quickly lost interest in the picnic as soon as Atlas left. "We can retire to the sitting room to talk some more if you'd like."

Zinnie packed up the picnic and handed the leftovers to Lucy. "Actually, I must be going now, too, I'm afraid. Thank you for a lovely afternoon."

Zinnie strolled down the cobblestone street toward the other side of the city. Her mind raced as she tried to figure out what she should do next.

She talked to Lela as the dragon hovered beside her at eye level.

"How can I spend time with Atlas without risking his father recognizing me? I'll have to keep him away from his home."

Lela zoomed in a circle and returned to the spot.

Zinnie kept brainstorming out loud. "But that could be a problem for me if others throughout the city recognize me. How is this going to work?"

She chewed on her thumbnail while she pondered.

"Zinnie, wait!"

Zinnie's heart skipped a beat when Atlas's voice called out to her.

Chapter 17

There was no use trying to hide. He had clearly spotted her.

Lela squeaked in her ear.

"I know. I can use this to my advantage," Zinnie agreed.

She stopped and turned around to greet him. She tried to hide her embarrassment. Although maybe a little of it showing could help her in this conversation.

"What happened?" Atlas quizzed her when he caught up. "I said I would be right back. Is everything alright? When you saw my father, you looked like you had seen a ghost!"

Zinnie tucked her hair behind her ears and gazed up at Atlas with her icy eyes. His steel gray ones almost glowed against his tanned skin and dark features. Her heart skipped a beat, and she allowed her eyelashes to flutter a little.

"Yes, sorry," she stammered on purpose.

Not because she had taken a half step closer to him and his nearness made her nervous. It was all part of her act, she convinced herself.

She kept her voice soft. "I was worried your father might be upset that you had a guest without his knowledge. I don't know what its like with your family, but the rules are pretty strict at my home." That wasn't a lie. "And you seem protective of his purpose for being here."

Atlas breathed a sigh of relief. "I understand. Our family is very relaxed about those kinds of things. My father is a bit picky about the care and protection of his maps, but he trusts Lucy and I to make wise choices about who we invite into our home and spend our time with. My only regret is that you didn't get to meet him at a time when he could have gotten to know you better. I know he would like you."

This time it was Atlas who rested his hand on Zinnie's upper arm. Her skin tingled beneath her sleeve from the connection. She made sure that Atlas noticed the warmth in her eyes.

"That's alright, Atlas. I'm sure I'll have the chance to meet him properly some time…"

"Yes, you will." He squeezed her arm and dropped his hand again. Her arm felt cold where his hand had just been. "I would love for you to join our family for dinner. He can tell you himself some of the stories behind the maps. Are you available?"

This caught Zinnie totally off guard. She had planned Atlas to be her mark, or rather Jessamine had planned it for her. But she didn't know if she could stomach tricking his entire family. It was already bad enough that his innocent younger sister had been roped into the whole thing. She had to find a way to decline his invitation. She settled for the truth. Sort of.

"I am so sorry, Atlas. I truly can't today. I must return home for supper tonight; my family is expecting me…"

"If not today, then when?" he insisted.

She found his persistence endearing.

No one else had ever worked so hard to have Zinnie join them for anything at all. Most people weren't exactly thrilled when she showed up, knowing that her mistress wanted something from them. Even the children that she tried to share her findings with didn't always trust her, knowing who she worked for.

She wanted to say yes to his invitation, but just couldn't bring herself to commit.

She shrugged.

"I will ask again. Soon." His warm smile lit up his face. "In the meantime…" It was his turn to give her a mischievous look.

She almost burst out laughing at how hard he had to try to look like that, but she managed to hold it in. Her eyes danced at the forced boyish expression on his face.

"In the meantime," he continued, "I request your assistance in showing me around the city. Helping me figure this place out." He threw his arms open wide and spun in a circle. "I'm afraid I will get lost if I don't have a proper guide." He returned to stand in front of her. Half a step closer than she had placed herself only moments before.

"Well? Will you do me the honor?" He reached a hand toward her and held it open.

She should jump at this opportunity. She'd be able to learn everything she needed to know. Surely receive another invitation into the home… without the rest of the family.

But a voice told her that she should tread carefully out and about in the city. They'd be better off getting to know one another indoors, at the library, or in a garden, not out here on the streets. So many things could go wrong…

But she couldn't resist his eager gaze.

She placed her hand in his. "I would be delighted."

And deep down inside, she truly meant it. That warmth spread up her arm again and went straight to her heart, which responded by speeding up its rhythm.

That same little voice reminded her that her end game was to steal something valuable from his family. That it was likely he would find out. At the very least after the job was accomplished, she would remove herself from interacting with him completely. They would not see one another again if she could help it.

Lela tugged on one of Zinnie's curls. She hovered by Zinnie's face and gave her a knowing look.

Zinnie shook her head ever so slightly. She widened her eyes and pinched her lips. She knew the danger in spending more time with Atlas. Her heart was on the line. She didn't need Lela to remind her.

By entertaining his good looks and sweet personality and allowing him to warm her from the inside out, she was only setting up herself, and probably him *and* his entire family, for heartbreak.

She told herself it was for a good reason. Whatever pain she may inflict upon them by her deception would be better than the physical harm that Jessamine had threatened.

She gritted her teeth and kept a sweet smile on her face.

True to her word, she spent the next three days with Atlas. She cut and styled her hair the same every morning, dressed in the same day dress she had acquired, adding a variety of trimmings to liven it up each day. She kept her innocent smile on her face and her worries locked away carefully in the back of her mind.

She told herself that she would gain Atlas's trust by playing tour guide, warming him up to her, and suggesting- with or without his knowledge- that they return to his home at some point. She'd find out where to find the map she needed. She'd steal it. The job would be over, and she could move on.

She showed Atlas all around the city during their time

together. Well, maybe not *everywhere*. There were some places that even she would not venture. She pointed those out to him from afar, instead.

And she certainly avoided the district where Jessamine's shop was located.

Lela worked great as a distraction when they needed to avoid eye contact, or worse, verbal contact, with anyone that might recognize either of them.

Atlas requested to see Zinnie's favorite places, and she chose a few she felt comfortable sharing.

Like the theater.

"The comedies they perform are spectacular. You should definitely make it a priority to see one!"

"I've read a lot of play-scripts in my studies, but mostly political stories or tragedies."

"What?" Zinnie scoffed. "Why in the world would you waste time on anything tragic? There's already so much to be sad about in the world. I like to stick to things that remind me to laugh."

He held out his hands in surrender. "I know, I know. But Father insists I be well-read and not waste time on frivolous entertainment."

"That pretty much sounds like a tragedy to me!" Zinnie commented. She clapped her hand over her mouth. "I'm sorry, Atlas, that was out of line."

He shook his head. "No, you're right. It is a sad tale. Perhaps you will take me to see a performance here sometime?"

She nodded but couldn't speak. She wanted to promise him she would. But she refused to make promises she could not keep.

Instead, she changed the subject. She kept her voice disarmingly cheerful and spoke quickly so that he wouldn't try to squeeze a promise from her about... well, about anything.

She filled him in on the long history of the city. How it had been originally founded by a retired pirate, named Dorian, of course, who wished to remain close to the sea and stay safe from those who would wish revenge upon him. Or try to steal his treasure.

"Soon the City of Dorian became a place of refuge for those seeking to leave their pasts behind. As you can guess, a lot of different characters came here, and over time the city grew. Since there's no extra land to spread outward, the city has grown upwards, instead."

Atlas soaked in all the information, just like Zinnie had hoped.

Once, a group of orphaned children called out to her. They waved her over. She kept a sweet smile on her lips as she approached with Atlas close by her side.

The children surrounded her. She offered them a few trinkets from her bag. One tugged on her arm to pull her down. She lowered herself and the child whispered something into her ear that had to do with Jessamine. She pulled away and giggled before the girl could finish her statement. She couldn't afford for Atlas to overhear anything.

The girl gave Zinnie a confused look.

Zinnie mouthed "later" to her.

The girl nodded and hugged Zinnie around the waist instead.

Atlas and Zinnie waved as they strolled away from the children.

"I served orphans in Elodale before we moved, too. They do tend to take a liking to you, don't they?" Atlas commented.

If he only knew, she thought.

Chapter 18

While Zinnie was busy keeping an eye on everything and everyone around them, employing her keen observation skills to make sure her cover was not compromised, Atlas's behavior didn't go unnoticed.

If she hadn't been so adept at paying attention to multiple things at once, she would have either slipped up concealing her true identity, or not noticed the way Atlas interacted with everyone around them.

When a woman at the market didn't have enough coin to pay for her entire purchase and became flustered searching her pocket for any spare change, Atlas stepped in and quietly slipped the vendor the necessary amount. The woman tried to thank him, but he waved away her apology and returned to Zinnie's side.

She kept her mouth closed but allowed her eyes to show her surprise and admiration.

A man dropped a coin purse heavy laden with money, and Atlas thought nothing of picking it up and chasing him down to return it. He could have easily kept it for himself, and no one would have been the wiser. *She* would probably have slipped it into her own pocket. Jessamine had always told her that once something had been lost, it no longer belonged to the original owner. It would rightfully belong to whomever discovered it. Guilt stabbed at her for all the times she had knowingly kept something that belonged to someone else, even if her intentions had never been bad.

As they strolled down one of the busier main streets with plenty of carriage and cart traffic headed in both directions, a ball rolled from an alley to their left. Atlas didn't hesitate to dodge the traffic, retrieve the ball, and return it to the grubby children playing in the shadows. And he didn't stop there. He kicked it around with them for a few minutes and waved goodbye when they left.

Zinnie didn't have time to play with the children she interacted with. She always had a mission to accomplish, information to deliver or discover discreetly, or something to "acquire" for her mistress.

Atlas held doors for her, as any gentleman would. But he also assisted others in carrying packages, holding doors, or offering a hand up or down from a carriage. His vocabulary consisted of so many ways to say please, thank you, and you're welcome, that it left Zinnie's head spinning. He even stooped to pick up litter and carry it to the nearest trash collection container.

His thoughtfulness towards everyone around him only left Zinnie feeling smaller and meaner than ever before. *She* only ever thought about her mistress's needs and how she could accomplish them. Or about someday escaping this dirty rotten place to never return.

A new fear mingled with her apprehension about Atlas's safety from Jessamine. How could someone so genuine and good survive in this den of dishonesty and greed? Would the city change him? Would *he* become hardened like everyone else?

She wanted to protect him from this place but had no idea how it could be done.

She must have worn her emotions on her sleeve because Atlas poked her arm.

"What's wrong, Zinnie?" He wore a worried expression.

She placed a smile back on her face and shook her head. "Oh, nothing. I just... feel like I forgot something? You know the feeling..."

He relaxed and a smile brightened his eyes once more. "I'm sure you'll remember. Want help jogging your memory?"

"No, that's alright. If it's important, it will come back to me."

"Very well. Tell me about your upbringing, Zinnie. Do you have siblings? What are your parents like? Is it too forward to suggest that I would like to meet them?" A blush crept up his neck.

He had not suggested anything romantic or inappropriate in his behavior towards her, and she believed he truly was just curious about her. Maybe a little interested, but nothing serious. Which was for the best. A *friendship* that led to the map would end up being better for him, and herself if she was being honest, than a fake romantic relationship.

She fumbled over her reply before composing herself. "My parents' lives were cut short when I was young..."

Lela settled on Zinnie's shoulder and cooed. She rubbed her feathered head against Zinnie's cheek to offer comfort.

"Oh, Zinnie." A new compassionate frown pulled on his mouth and eyes. "I am so sorry." He rested his warm hand on her upper arm, sending tingles down her spine again.

"It was a long time ago. My… aunt," she settled for half-truths, calling Jessamine her aunt, "took me in and has seen to it that I receive the best education and plenty of opportunities to better my situation."

He shook his head. "That is so fortunate that you had her." His eyes swung to the dark alley beside them where they both knew orphaned children and teenagers hid from the authorities.

She knew what he was thinking. *That* could have been her life. And he was right. For how loveless her life with Jessamine had been, *was still*, she could have had it so much worse.

"I have no siblings, so it's just been me and my… aunt… since I was small. It's truly a disappointing story. There isn't really much else to tell. I'd much rather hear about your family! What was it like to travel so far?"

"Lucy and I have always been close, and the trip only strengthened our bond. Being in a new place and not knowing anyone, I am so glad to have her as a friend."

Zinnie nodded and smiled. "I've never traveled outside the city myself. How does one pass the time on a trip like that?"

Atlas chuckled. "Lucy and I played a lot of games during our journey. She has a knack for inventing good ones that don't require anything besides our minds."

Zinnie raised her eyebrows. "Really? Like what?" This was all new to her and she was truly eager to hear his reply.

"One she calls 'I Spy.' One person chooses something to 'spy' and the other must ask questions to figure out what it might be."

At the word "spy" Zinnie stiffened. But she quickly relaxed when she understood the context of the word. He didn't suspect anything about her. She must keep it that way.

"That sounds fun, I'd like to try!"

He laughed again.

"Please?" She playfully touched his arm.

He nodded. "You first."

"Alright." She looked around and gave him an innocent smile. "What am I supposed to do, exactly?"

He leaned down a little so he could look at their surroundings at her eye level and rested a hand on her upper back. "Choose something that you can see. Try to make it difficult for me to guess, something that I wouldn't expect or might have trouble noticing."

He kept his hand pressed gently against her. It was quite distracting. She normally was astutely observant but had trouble focusing on anything other than his nearness, his breath in her ear. His deep voice.

She gulped and randomly chose something.

"Alright, I've got something."

He stood again and removed his hand. She wilted at the loss of his nearness and touch but didn't allow her feelings to show.

"Now you say, 'I spy with my pretty blue eye something…' and give me a clue. It's color, size, smell, anything that would allow me to guess without making it too easy."

Her heart skipped a beat when she heard him say the color of her eyes. He had noticed. Many people weren't aware of the eye color of those around them, and her eye color was not anything unique or striking. Not like his silver eyes that shone against his tanned complexion and black hair.

Pull yourself together, Zinnie, she scolded herself.

"I think I get it," she said out loud. "I spy with my eye something… lacy." She chose the word carefully.

"Now I look around and try to use your clue to guess

what it is." He squinted his eyes and studied their surroundings.

"You're never going to guess," she teased.

"Shush," he countered with a grin. "The fabric over there?" He pointed across the way toward a hat shop.

"Nope."

A couple more failed guesses and he shrugged. "I give up!"

"What? Just like that? Use your observation skills, Atlas. I said it was lacy, not made of lace. Keep looking around. Look in every *nook and cranny*..." she emphasized the last words.

He looked around again, but away from the shops and people and at the buildings and corners instead.

"The... spiderweb?" He gave her an uncertain look.

She clapped her hands once. "Yes! Well done!"

"Oh, you *are* good at this game. Let's see if I can stump you this time!" His voice rang with excitement as he tried to spot something that she wouldn't be able to guess.

She watched his face carefully and knew the moment he had settled on something by the way his eyes paused, squinted, and continued to pretend to look at other things.

He gave his clue. "I spy something..." He pretended to think.

She smirked inwardly at his trying-to-be-sneaky voice. He wasn't very good at subterfuge, was he? She grinned at his handsome face.

"...*shadowy*." He folded his arms and gave her a triumphant smile.

"Oh, you are making this difficult, aren't you?" She held his gaze. "Is it the parasol stand?" She didn't break their locked eyes to look.

His jaw dropped open and his eyes widened. "What? *How?*" He stammered. He looked around at the parasol stand to make sure it was still in the same place. "You didn't even look around! How did you know?"

She couldn't wipe the grin off her face now if she had wanted to. She turned and strolled down the lane again.

He jogged to catch up. "Zinnie! How did you do that? Can you read my mind or something?"

He stood in front of her and folded his arms. "Are you part Forest Person? Can you talk to animals? Did Lela tell you? How did you do it?" Laughter crinkled his eyes, but astonishment kept his face in a surprised expression.

"Wouldn't you like to know." She teased in a sing-songy voice, side stepped around him, and continued her leisurely stroll.

This was too much fun. He was so easy to tease. So trusting, gullible…

Her heart squeezed. He was *too* trusting. He really shouldn't even trust her if he knew the truth about her reasons for befriending him.

I'm a horrible person. The words filled her mind, gripped her chest, and settled like a rock in her stomach.

Atlas gently wrapped his fingers around her upper arm. The touch, so tender and sweet, made her shiver. She hid her reaction from him and made sure her face still reflected the fun she was supposed to be having. She was sure it didn't reach her eyes, but Atlas was too distracted to notice.

"Would you truly like me to teach you?" she asked him.

"And be able to win at 'I Spy' with Lucy *every time*? Absolutely!" He hopped on the balls of his feet while he waited for her to pretend to deliberate.

She tapped her finger against her chin, just below her smirk, and she stretched her smile wide.

"Alright, I'll do it. Follow me."

She grabbed his hand and dragged him across the street toward the parasol stand.

Chapter 19

Atlas held the paper cone of sugared roasted nuts toward Zinnie. His feet swung back and forth from his perch atop the low stone wall near the central garden of the city.

"Don't mind if I do," she said sweetly as she pinched a pair of nuts between her fingers.

She tossed one of the nuts in the air and Lela zipped upward to catch it in her mouth before it began its descent.

Atlas laughed at Lela's antics. He said to Zinnie, "If you don't eat more than one at a time there won't be any left." He popped a handful of nuts into his mouth and moaned at their warm sweetness. "I promise, I'm not going to slow down just so you can be ladylike…"

Zinnie blushed. He was so cute the way he acted as if he had never tasted anything so good before.

She placed one in her mouth, ladylike, like he said. They were delicious. But his company was the warm, sweet part that she relished, not the snack.

"Tell me again how you pulled it off?" He crumpled up the sticky paper and held it in one hand, ready to discard it in the proper way when he had the chance. "How did you get my watch from my pocket without me noticing?" His voice sounded incredulous. He pinned admiring eyes onto her face and studied her, as if she would somehow give it away if he looked hard enough.

She looked away; afraid he might learn the truth about her if he looked too carefully.

"I told you." She tucked a loose strand of curls behind her ear. "I twirled the parasol as a distraction and focused your attention on its design. I leaned forward and placed my hand on your arm so you would be aware that I touched you. Then I switched hands on the parasol, slipped my other hand into your pocket, pinched the chain between my fingers," she demonstrated like her fingers were the blades on a pair of scissors, "and slid the watch from your pocket. It's simple, really…"

He laughed out loud. "You make it sound simple, but it is truly like magic. And you're *sure* it's not magic?" He tilted his head and squinted at her in a playful way.

It was her turn to laugh now. "No, I assure you, sleight of hand is *not* magic."

The laughter died down and he studied her again, a little more serious this time. "I don't understand how you know how to do it, though. This isn't something they teach in etiquette classes for *all* ladies, is it?" A surprised look raised his eyebrows.

"No." She giggled and covered her mouth with one hand. "I told you; I was bored as a kid."

"And your family never took you out of the City of Dorian?" he shook his head. "I don't get it."

She shrugged and the fib rolled smoothly off her tongue. "They aren't much for traveling, I guess."

A thoughtful expression crossed his face. "I've heard

rumors that some people can't leave the City of Dorian." He gave her a quizzical look.

She managed to keep a neutral expression on her face. "I've heard that, too."

He leaned closer and spoke in a quieter tone. "I've also heard that the secret enchantments that keep some people here can't be broken."

She nodded. "That's my understanding."

He had *no* idea. She would give *anything* to be able to break whatever spell kept her locked in this city. Her stomach flipped but she kept up her calm façade.

He looked at her sideways as if waiting for her reaction.

"What other rumors have you heard?" She teased to ease the subtle tension.

He leaned back and looked at the sky. "That the enchantments don't extend *beneath* the city. At least, that's what the city leaders say."

She tipped her head. "But we're high above the beach. Why would it matter if the enchantment didn't work beneath the city? It's too far to escape."

"Wouldn't descending on a long rope do the trick?"

"No, I don't think so… It's… much too far." She must not allude to the fact that she had already tried to escape through her sink hole with rope. It hadn't worked. The barrier had been as invisible as ever and as firm as a stone. But that was a long time ago…

"There has to be a way, though, right?" Atlas continued. "I mean, otherwise why would people say it?"

Zinnie fought to not roll her eyes. People said all kinds of things, it didn't make any of them true. She of course was the prime example of this. Half the things she said or implied were false, weren't they?

"Although, they did say something about requiring something enchanted in order to break the barrier. I guess like a double negative? But who ever heard of enchanted rope?" He grinned, which enhanced his dimples.

The charming look almost distracted her from what he had just said. Her hair was enchanted. Could she use her *hair* as enchanted rope? Could it be that simple?

She reminded herself that she had a job to get done. She couldn't be thinking about anything else. She would investigate this new idea once Jessamine had the map.

Speaking of maps… She pulled her thoughts back to her task at hand.

"Tell me more about Elodale. Your father collected maps; he must have traveled a bit?"

Atlas nodded.

"Why come here? Did you not like it there?"

"No, we liked it just fine. Some scouts from Dorian sent by the leaders came to Elodale. They perused Father's collection and asked him what it would take for him to relocate. I guess they wanted access to his collection."

Zinnie put a thoughtful expression on her face now. More intentional than Atlas's, of course. "Why do you think they want to see his maps? Are they looking for something?"

And why does Jessamine want that specific one? She couldn't ask him the question, but maybe she'd be able to figure it out on her own.

Atlas waved his hand in the air. "Who knows? I have no interest in politics. Frankly, I'm surprised my father even agreed to come. But they convinced him, somehow."

"Huh." Zinnie tapped her chin. "Do any of his maps lead to treasure?"

She couldn't help but think of the telltale "X" that Jessamine had mentioned.

Atlas laughed. "I doubt it. Otherwise, we'd be much wealthier, wouldn't we?"

Zinnie cringed. Compared to her own lifestyle, the Forster's had wealth beyond her wildest dreams!

"Enough about maps… show me another trick?" His eyes gleamed.

She pretended to ponder the idea and shook her head.

"Please?" He blinked at her and showed off his dimples again.

In her mind she readily agreed but made him think she wasn't interested.

Before he could assist her off the wall, she slid to the ground.

He was so insistent on helping her down that he clambered off the wall to lend her a hand.

"If most young women don't learn the skills you have acquired, then why did you?" He held her hand in one of his.

She willed herself to remain calm and collected so he wouldn't see her nerves at his gentle touch. She fiddled with her sleeves to distract him from her reaction. "When you have no siblings and all the grown ups around you are busy doing grown up stuff, you find ways to distract yourself…"

"What about a different hobby? Like stitching?" he asked.

She gave him a dead pan look. "Seriously? Do you know how boring stitching is? A girl can only stitch so many samplers before she feels as though her mind is turning into mush."

He nodded thoughtfully. "I suppose…"

"But the stitching did help my fingers become quite nimble…"

She raised her hand to his shoulder height. His pocket watch, pinched by the chain between two of her knuckles, swayed in front of him. The light of the setting sun glinted off its intricate carved designs.

"Incredible!" His face beamed. "You amaze me, Zinnie! And I want you to teach me to do *this*, too."

She grinned. "I don't know. A magician never reveals her secrets…"

"*Not* magic, though, remember?" He tugged a curl that hung beside her face and let it spring back up again.

She met his gaze.

He froze and locked his eyes onto hers. His eyes flicked to look at her mouth and back to her eyes.

She blushed and lowered her eyes to emphasize her long, dark lashes.

He swallowed when she met his gaze again. "The hour grows late." His voice sounded strained. "I should make sure you travel home safely."

She smiled shyly at him. "If you insist."

She allowed him to escort her to a building on the opposite side of town from where she actually lived.

Lela clicked in her ear to scold her, but it's not like Zinnie had a choice in the matter. She couldn't exactly show him where she really lived, now could she?

It didn't take long. Atlas and Zinnie walked in silence.

Her heart sped up at his new nearness. When his arm brushed hers, she blushed.

He ran his fingers through his hair and glanced sideways at her from time to time until they arrived at her "home."

"Goodnight, Zinnie." He nodded at her and gazed into her eyes.

"Goodnight, Atlas." Her voice came out a little breathier than usual.

She told herself it was all part of the act. But the flipping of her stomach argued that point with her head.

Zinnie groaned and threw her arm over her face in her prone position on her bed.

"What am I going to do, Lela? I've already taken too long at obtaining the map. Every time the opportunity arises, something interrupts.

"And it doesn't help that when he looks at me, I'm weak at the knees. When his hand lingers on mine it makes me want to grab it and never let go. I miss him when he's not with me, and I can't wait to see him again.

"I'm not supposed to *actually* fall for him. I've only known him a couple of weeks and have spent very little time with him, but I feel as though I know him better than anyone!"

Lela released a puff of steam and clicked her sharp teeth together.

"Except you, of course," Zinnie insisted.

"And now what he said about the enchantment being able to be fooled by a second enchantment? What if he's right? What if it worked and I could lower myself right out of the city with my own hair?"

The idea seemed too good to be true. She struggled to believe it and told herself not to get her hopes up at the same time.

Lela winged in a circle overhead. An iridescent feather floated down and landed on Zinnie's arm.

She picked it off with her other hand and twirled it between her fingers. The light reflected off it like a rainbow. Her eyes went out of focus, and she imagined showing the feather to Atlas.

Her less-than-honest side calculated how she could use it as an excuse to talk about Lela. She could ask him where he thought the dragon came from. It would be easy to turn the conversation toward maps.

Then her heart took over. She imagined his smiling lips, those cute dimples in his cheeks. The laugh lines around his breathtaking steel eyes.

She groaned. "How am I supposed to trick him into showing me, and maybe even giving me, the map Mistress wants if I can't stop thinking about his handsome face?"

She released the feather and let it float to the floor. She squeezed her eyes shut, only to see his eyes gazing down at her, hearing his laughter ring in her ears, watching him extend kindness and gentleness to everyone around him, including herself.

She abruptly stood. "I don't deserve someone like him. He certainly deserves someone *way* better than me."

How could she use her head to accomplish this task when her heart was in danger of falling for her mark?

Chapter 20

She paced back and forth, her hands gesturing wildly as she spoke to Lela, but really to herself. "I should just investigate his idea about using my hair as rope and figure out how to escape now. Cut off ties before we both end up heartbroken."

She walked three steps across the room, turned on her heels, and rebutted her own declaration.

"But what about the full moon? What is Jessamine planning? I need to get this job finished, then I can worry about myself."

Three more steps, faster this time. Turn.

"Whatever Jessamine has planned probably isn't as bad as it seems. Right? What could she *really* do to them?"

Zinnie's hands waved in the air. Her pace quickened. Her heart raced.

"But I *know* she is capable of things beyond my imagination. I don't really know her. What if she is truly dangerous? Evil?"

"But she's never done anything to harm *me* before, right? Would she really hurt Atlas's family for some old piece of parchment?"

"She hasn't done anything to harm me… *yet*. She only keeps me safe because she uses my abilities for her own gain."

"What am I going to do?" She shouted the final words, then slapped her hands over her mouth and snapped her head to look at the door.

What would Jessamine do if she knew how conflicted Zinnie really was about the assignment? She would probably just lock Zinnie in her room again and get the map *"by whatever means necessary."*

A shiver ran down Zinnie's spine. And not a pleasant one like when Atlas's hand lingered on her arm. Or his eyes on her lips.

She squeezed her eyes shut and clenched her fists. She had to stay focused. Get this job over with. She couldn't waste more time!

A loud rap on her door made her jump so high both feet left the floor.

"Zinnie, I must speak with you. Please open the door at once." Mistress Jessamine's voice sounded harsh and impatient through the rough wooden door.

"Coming." Why did she even say that? She rolled her eyes at herself. Two steps carried her there and she yanked the door open.

Jessamine looked past Zinnie into her room. "Are you speaking to someone?" She pinned her eyes on Zinnie's face and frowned.

"No! Only to myself. I promise!" Zinnie wrung her hands together. Had Jessamine heard any of the one-sided conversation about Zinnie's conflicted feelings? Or about the thoughts she entertained of escape?

"I'm assuming you still have not made progress on your assignment?"

Zinnie lowered her gaze and shook her head. She wanted to tell her about the progress that she had made, but when Jessamine said "progress", she only wanted results. Anything else would be seen as an excuse.

"I assumed as much. You really are losing your touch."

Zinnie fumbled for something to say.

Before she could, Jessamine spoke again. "I have a job that needs to be done tomorrow. You will need to put aside any other plans and accomplish this for me." Her voice was sharp and her gaze sharper.

Zinnie swallowed the lump in her throat. "What… what is the assignment?"

The ominous tone from her mistress made her nervous. Was Jessamine giving up on Zinnie's task with Atlas? Was she going to make Zinnie do something rash in order to obtain the map? Was she as dangerous as Zinnie now feared?

"A shipment of phoenix ashes?" Zinnie murmured the words to Lela, hidden beneath her thick braid that stretched to her midback beneath her dark cloak. "What could she want with phoenix ashes?"

Jessamine's insistence that Zinnie perform this extra task only set her behind schedule to retrieve the map even more. She had to accomplish this new assignment as quickly as possible so she could meet up with Atlas again. She must get the map. Soon!

Lela squeaked at Zinnie as if to answer her question.

"I know she said it's because the person who has them owes her a debt. Goodness knows nearly everyone in this city owes Jessamine something or pays her to keep their secrets. But why *this*? Why not something… less dangerous?"

The only things phoenix ashes could be used for were fast

burning fires that left no trace, harmful explosives, and poison.

Zinnie dodged the vulture rabbits huddled around their prey in the street and hurried around the corner near the gnomish clockmaker. She checked both directions before she slipped through a dirty, smelly alley behind the aquarist and disappeared into the shadows.

She had told Atlas she didn't have magic, and it was true. People only saw what they wanted to see.

If she was quiet, unremarkable, and kept to herself, people ignored her presence more often than not. When she did get stopped or questioned, she showed off her pretty blond hair and acted innocent. No one suspected a delicate girl like herself to be up to no good. Even in a place like the City of Dorian.

Frankly, that's how Jessamine could get away with so much, too. The woman never seemed to age, and she could play the innocent part just as well as Zinnie. In fact, she's the one who modeled the behavior for Zinnie during her training. And she had been an efficient mentor.

"All right, Lela. You stay here. You know what to do if someone comes." Lela perched on a high ledge just outside a narrow door in the rough exterior of the building. Zinnie checked for onlookers again before she expertly cracked the lock, slid through the door, and closed it without so much as a click.

The dragon would cause a ruckus if anyone approached, which would allow Zinnie time to retreat into the shadows or make a hasty exit another way.

She hated to use Lela like that. If the dragon was captured, she would be sent right back to the menagerie at the palace and Zinnie would never see her again. But at times like these when Mistress Jessamine was so on edge, Zinnie didn't have much choice. If *she* were caught, *she* would end up in the dungeons. Or worse, used in one of Jessamine's mysterious "projects."

Her mistress always seemed to be up to something sinister, and she had just learned it involved the dungeon. And hazardous phoenix ashes, apparently. She couldn't risk getting caught. Besides, Lela always insisted on helping.

Zinnie tiptoed through the storage space behind the office of the distributor. The man didn't keep his items out for everyone to see. No, he kept them locked away in the back of the building.

This is where Zinnie would find the phoenix ashes that Jessamine so desperately wanted.

Did she plan to use them to steal the map? Did it involve physical harm to the Forester's? Or was it for an entirely different purpose altogether? She hoped that whatever it was, it didn't involve Atlas's family.

She picked through the crates and barrels but didn't see any sign of the ashes. She let out a huff and turned in a slow circle.

"If I was a broker of smuggled items, where would I hide phoenix ashes so that they would be impossible to find?" She tapped her chin and narrowed her eyes.

A layer of dust coated many of the items in the room, but a fresh disturbance in the dust left a neat trail into the far corner of the room.

"Aha!"

She followed the trail to a box expertly camouflaged in the shadows by an equally dusty tarpaulin.

"Very clever." She nodded, impressed.

She pushed the tarpaulin back and found her quarry.

"Mistress Jessamine said to remove one carton and leave this… disturbingly threatening… note behind." She shuddered and remembered why she obeyed her mistress each and every time she received an assignment.

"Here goes." She removed the palm sized carton. A quick

peek inside confirmed the contents. She slipped the box into her satchel, put the folded-up parchment in its place, and restored the tarpaulin to its original position.

"I wonder how long it will take before he notices that note?" she whispered.

Making sure her feet had left no footprints to show she had been there, she slipped out the door again into the alley, retrieved Lela from her perch, and stuffed her satchel containing the highly combustible phoenix ashes beneath her cloak for safe keeping.

She zig-zagged her way through the city and beat a hasty retreat to Jessamine's shop.

"I hope she's there so I can give this to her and receive permission to continue with my 'Atlas mission,'" she murmured to Lela.

Today's goal would be to find her way back into their house. Figure out where the map in question was being stored. And either convince Atlas to give it to her- or let her "borrow" it- or make a plan to steal it. By the end of the day, one way or another, she would have the map. Not only to appease Jessamine, but to protect the innocent lives at stake. She would not allow anything to stop her this time.

As if right on cue, the man she couldn't keep out of her thoughts materialized in front of her in the street.

"Eeep!" She squealed and ducked behind the awning of a shabby bakery. She secured her hood to hide her telltale blond locks and peeked around the corner to observe the object of her daydreams.

Lela peeked her head out, too. She cooed into Zinnie's ear.

Atlas turned his head around. Could he have heard Lela over the ruckus of the city?

Zinnie ducked out of sight again.

When she felt that a sufficient amount of time had passed, she peeked over her shoulder and begged Lela to stay silent.

Atlas carried a large basket over one arm and appeared to be looking for something.

A picnic? In this part of town?

Her thoughts went over every scenario. A picnic didn't make sense. Unless he was looking for someone to take on a picnic? Could he have known to find her here?

No one knew she was here! Except Jessamine. Could the woman have set Zinnie up for failure? Did she know that Zinnie had developed feelings for Atlas?

Now it was Zinnie's turn to make a noise, though hers was less of a coo and more of a moan of desperation.

Just then, Atlas spotted whomever or whatever he appeared to be searching for. His smile widened, and he took purposeful steps down the street the opposite way from where Zinnie hid.

She let out a sigh of relief. Then something pricked her heart. She frowned.

"Lela, where could he be going? Who could he be meeting?" She tried to hide her jealousy from her tiny friend.

It didn't work. The dragon nipped at Zinnie's hair and tugged.

Zinnie gave her a sideways glance. "I know I shouldn't care. And I know we're in a hurry, but…"

She couldn't help herself. She padded down the street, staying close to the shadows and walls, and followed Atlas.

Chapter 21

Why is he going in *there*?" she started to ask Lela. Then her breath caught in her throat. "Oh!" The word came out as a whisper.

The place he entered was a group home for widows and orphans. The sweating sickness that had overtaken the city over the previous months still lingered in places like this.

"Lela, why would he go into a place like that?" She crept up to the window and peered through the dingy pane of glass.

Atlas moved around the front room, offering savory bread and sweet rolls to those who convalesced in the chairs and beds.

"He's risking his own health by being in there," she hissed. Her breath fogged the window. She ducked and allowed the mist to clear, before rising to look again.

He rested a hand on a woman's shoulder. He patted a child atop her straight, dark braids.

"He could have sent a servant. Or a runner, even." Zinnie no longer pretended to be talking to Lela. She talked to herself. For real this time. Sincerely analyzing the situation and why Atlas would do something of the sort.

She was so caught up in her own thoughts, that she didn't realize he had finished visiting the people and handing out treats. He took quick steps toward the entrance just beside Zinnie.

The door swung open. Zinnie was about to come face to face with this incredibly generous man who did not deserve to be treated the way that Jessamine had forced Zinnie to treat him.

She froze.

Lela flew into Atlas's face and flapped her feathery wings.

Zinnie took the moment to skirt around the side of the building and crouched beside a smelly basket of soiled laundry.

She heard Atlas's reaction to the dragon from her hiding place.

"Lela? What are you doing here?" Atlas spoke in a soothing manner, likely in an attempt to calm Lela from her wild flapping and hot breath. "Is Zinnie with you?"

His footsteps indicated he walked in Zinnie's direction. She covered herself with her cloak completely and leaned against the laundry. She could not be caught here. Not with the item she hid beside her body. Not looking like this…

Lela must have convinced him with her fire or her wings to not continue in Zinnie's direction.

Zinnie made a mental note to find a treat for Lela that would express her extreme gratitude for not giving away Zinnie's location.

The sounds of the man's feet and the dragon's chirps dissipated.

Zinnie waited a little longer than necessary to emerge from her hiding place. She peeked around the corner. The pair were nowhere in sight.

Zinnie made her way home as fast as possible, reveling in her good fortune in having Lela by her side, and pouring over the why's of Atlas doing what he had done.

The more she turned all those thoughts over in her head, the sicker she felt. Was she a terrible person? Jessamine *made* her do the things she did. She didn't have a choice in the matter.

Did she?

Her feet carried her past the normal turn toward Jessamine's shop. Her mind bounced back and forth between the plan to steal the map from the Foresters' and the idea that she might have a way to escape after all.

The rumors swirled. Escape beneath the city? Use her hair as rope? Had she been saving her hair all this time for just such a purpose? Could she really be that fortunate?

By the time Lela caught up to her, she found herself on the ground behind the feathercorn stables, peering through the sinkhole.

"What do you think, Lela? Could it really be true?"

Lela circled above Zinnie, who hovered above the hole.

"I need some hair to test the theory."

Zinnie pulled her scissors from her pouch. She released the braid from beneath her cloak, pulled it as taught as she could, and cut it right there in the street. If anyone saw her, they might think her a foolish girl. But what choice did she have? She had to know.

Lela huffed smoke in her direction.

"I'll be careful, Lela, I promise."

Zinnie expertly weaved the arms-length lock into a tight rope. She attached it to a piece of rope from the stable and attached that rope to one of the support beams of the structure nearby.

She lowered the hair through the hole. Locked eyes with Lela. She clenched her fists and her jaw and gripped the rope with both hands.

"Here goes nothing."

Lela flew in fast circles around her. The panic she displayed did not go unnoticed to Zinnie. She knew the risk just as well as her tiny friend. If the rope failed… she wouldn't think about the disastrous results…

Zinnie's feet slipped through the hole. Her legs and torso went next. She held the edge of the sink hole with one hand and the rope with the other. She tugged on the makeshift rope. It felt sturdy enough.

One last inhale and exhale, and Zinnie gripped the rope with both hands. It bore all her weight now. She squeezed her eyes shut and waited for the worst.

The rope held. She sighed and lowered herself as far as she dared on the short length of hair rope.

When she had tried this years ago, she might as well have stood on a solid floor beneath the sink hole. But this time she sank below that point with absolutely no resistance.

Her heart leapt. "It's working, Lela! I can't believe it!"

She dangled for another moment or two before she pulled herself back into the City of Dorian.

"I can't believe I've lived here all this time, spread and received countless rumors, and the nice new boy that shows up out of the blue was the one to discover this secret! I wonder if he heard it from the city leaders themselves? If people knew, Lela… can you imagine?"

She pulled the hair-rope through the hole, detached it from the feathercorn stable, and stashed it in her satchel beside the phoenix ashes.

"The ashes!" Zinnie gasped.

She stared longingly at the sink hole. If she had been conflicted before, she was even more so now.

"I don't have time to waste. If I'm gone too long…"

She could only imagine the punishment she might receive from Jessamine if the woman thought she had cheated her or not retrieved the ashes. She would not be able to finish the mission with the map if she was locked in her room again.

"The hole will have to wait until later. But we will come back and make a plan, Lela. This is it! We are finally going to escape, once and for all!"

She bounced home on light feet, imagining all the things she would do with her imminent freedom.

The further from the hole she went, though, the weight of what she must accomplish first returned. The guilt gnawed at her insides until she arrived at the shop.

"You do not look well, child," Jessamine taunted. She folded her arms and leaned away from Zinnie as if she was afraid to catch whatever Zinnie had come down with. "Did you manage to get the *item* before you decided to become ill? Or did you fail like your task with the map? Do I need to assign you something easier for your little head?"

"No, ma'am." Zinnie thrust the box of ashes toward her mistress and hurried past her to her room.

She did feel ill, but not with the sweating sickness or a stomach flu.

Her mind and heart battled one another, worse than ever before.

Should she try to escape the city? She might just have enough hair saved beneath her bed to accomplish the task, though the distance to the beach below was great…

Should she steal the map for Jessamine? The woman's actions lately left Zinnie fearing her more than ever. What was the woman up to? Was Zinnie a bad person for helping her accomplish whatever her evil purposes may be?

And what about the Forster's? If Zinnie didn't steal the map they would be placed directly in Jessamine's path.

"Ugh, Lela! Why does it have to be so hard to do the right thing?"

Lela cooed in response and fluffed her feathers.

"You're right. I'll just have to focus on one thing at a time. I can't worry about Jessamine's plans. I must simply do what I can to protect the Forester's, even if that means stealing the map. Then we can make our escape."

Something in her heart twinged. What about the feelings she denied having for Atlas? Whether or not she admitted to herself, let alone anyone else, they were there.

She pushed the thoughts aside. *You'll just have to deal with that later, Zinnie. For now, you have a job to do.*

Her heart seemed to answer, *But it's not fair.*

Her head responded. *Life isn't fair, it never has been. Not for someone as corrupt as you.* Jessamine's words that she had drilled into Zinnie's head her whole life filled her with shame.

Nausea roiled in her stomach.

Before she allowed herself to flop onto her bed and melt into a puddle of self-pity, she reopened her satchel and pulled the makeshift rope from inside. She held it in her hands.

Her freedom lay at the edge of the city. It was so close…

She yanked the case from beneath her bed and threw open the lid. She pulled out all the strands, braids, and twists. She added the knew length to it and stretched it in a great spiral around the perimeter of her tiny room.

She sat back on her heels and calculated in her head.

"Do you think it's enough?" she asked Lela.

The dragon only watched from her perch atop Zinnie's mirror.

Zinnie examined the length carefully with her eyes. Recalled the distance to the beach below the city. It just might be enough. She could leave. Now. Never look back.

Her heart sank and she squeezed her eyes closed. She willed her tears to stay inside her head and not leak down her cheeks like they wanted to.

She breathed in and out several times to master her emotions and counted on her fingers.

"Only fifteen days until the full moon. I *will* get the map." The words came out between clenched teeth. "I *will* deliver it to Jessamine. And then I will *leave*." She eyed the hair rope once more and carefully stored it beneath her bed again.

When she stood, she caught her reflection in the mirror. She would pay the price for cutting her hair in haste like she had done.

"It's a mess! It will take the rest of the day to grow this back out again." She raked her fingers through her too short hair and sighed in defeat. "I suppose we'll have to wait until tomorrow to see Atlas… I mean, continue the mission."

Zinnie blushed and looked away from her reflection. "I'll just stay in today and do chores. Just in case…"

She couldn't run the risk of Atlas seeing her like this. Jessamine would find plenty of things for her to do around their home while she waited for her hair to grow back out again.

Zinnie smoothed the pale blue fabric with her hands along the front of her expensive daytime outfit.

She whispered to Lela. "Do you see him? Is he coming?"

The dragon hovered in the air and gazed in the direction of Atlas's home. A moment later she swooped toward Zinnie and perched on her shoulder.

"Alright. Let's get this job done."

Chapter 22

*J*ust as she had expected, her hair had grown to the appropriate length overnight and she had styled it so that it would look the same to Atlas as it had during all their previous encounters.

When should I tell him about my hair? What will he think? He'll surely think I'm magic then, won't he?

She smirked to herself and allowed the pleased expression to linger on her face.

The reality was, she would never tell him about her hair. She would retrieve the map as soon as possible. Maybe even that day. Then she would escape this place forever.

Her heart ached at the thought of leaving him behind, but at least he would be safe from Jessamine.

As dishonest as everyone else in the place was, that woman was by far the worst. Especially with the things Zinnie had seen and heard lately.

Phoenix ashes? The dungeon?

Vicious creatures?

The full moon?

Atlas and his family would know how to protect themselves from the more obvious deceptive people they would encounter here.

And Jessamine would have no reason to do business with them again.

She hoped.

"*It's true*," she told herself. And she must force herself to believe it.

Her heart skipped a beat when Atlas appeared from around the corner.

"Show time," she murmured to Lela.

She walked forward and pretended to be looking at something on the opposite side of the street from Atlas. Before he could notice her presence, she brushed against his arm.

"Oh! I'm so sorr… Atlas!" She allowed her voice to fill with pure joy at seeing him. It wasn't as much of an act as it was the truth, but she shoved those feelings away. "Fancy bumping into you here!"

Atlas tugged at his burgundy brocade waistcoat. His whole face lit up upon recognizing who had startled him.

"Zinnie!" His eyes darted to Lela as she zoomed after an insect snack. He returned his gaze to Zinnie. "I saw Lela yesterday out by herself? Is everything alright? I feared you were ill…" He furrowed his brow and appraised her appearance as if he might be able to see an outward indication of why she had been absent from Lela's presence the day before.

Zinnie allowed herself to giggle in a sweet way at his reaction. She rested her hand on his upper arm and squeezed. "I assure you I am perfectly well!" She allowed her hand to linger.

Atlas's throat bobbed and his smile returned. His shoulders relaxed. "That is great news!"

She blushed.

He shuffled his feet and kept his eyes locked onto hers.

She had never, *ever* been stumped for words before,

especially when on a job.

"Did you…" Zinnie blurted at the same time that Atlas said, "I was wondering…"

They both laughed out loud and the tension between them disappeared.

Lela returned just then.

Atlas invited the dragon to perch on his hand. Lela accepted and fluffed her feathers to capture his attention.

Zinnie grinned at her tiny friend's antics. The dragon liked Atlas as much as Zinnie did. Which was probably why she always gave Zinnie disapproving looks whenever she had to further the con with Atlas.

"You first, of course." Atlas gestured at Zinnie to speak.

"Did you try playing 'I Spy' with Lucy?" She motioned for Lela to return to her own shoulder.

Atlas's eyes twinkled.

Zinnie wanted to melt right there on the street at the new mischief she saw behind them. She forced herself to not reveal the feelings that were welling up inside of her but keep a calm façade.

"Yes!" He had already begun to answer. "I totally won every round, too. One guess. Every time. She was blown away!" He waved his hands around and the delight on his face was nearly enough to make Zinnie wrap her arms around him right in the middle of the street.

She refrained. It would not be proper. Besides, she couldn't remember the last time she had embraced, or been embraced, by anyone.

Her heart sank but she kept the warm smile on her face. Just being near him felt like a warm embrace. If his arms ever actually encircled her, her heart might actually explode.

Her lips twitched at the thought.

"What? What's so funny?" Atlas noticed her smirk.

Her cheeks flushed in an instant. "What? Oh! Nothing!"

"Come on," he pressed with a gleam in his eye.

"No!" She giggled. "No." She composed herself. Again.

Her heart fluttered. Again.

She allowed the feeling to show on her face and promised herself she would use the feelings to get the map.

And, she thought, *to not allow myself to get too caught up in all of the flirting. I need to be able to escape and have no reason to look back.*

"You were about to say something to me…"

She looped her hand through his arm and turned so they could stroll down the road, side by side. She pressed her upper arm against his and her hand pressed firmly enough on his arm so that he would feel it through his sleeves.

"I was about to say something?" He stammered and stared at her.

She returned the gaze.

He swallowed. "Oh! Yes! I was!" He laughed at his own distraction.

"Well, what is it?" She allowed her voice to reflect her sincere eagerness at hearing what he wanted to say to her.

"Yes. Well," he tripped over his words again.

He's nervous. The thought hit her like a brick wall. Her heart skipped a beat and giddiness rose up the back of her neck, leaving goosebumps on her arms beneath her sleeves.

"I was wondering," he continued. "Would you do me the honor of joining our family for dinner tomorrow evening?"

Now it was Zinnie's turn to trip. But not over her words. Over her actual feet.

Lela let out a miniscule flaming screech when Zinnie stumbled, which stung Zinnie's ear inside and out.

Atlas shot his arm around her back and gripped her side to keep her from falling. His other hand reached forward and took her hand to support her from the front, too.

"Zinnie! Are you alright?" He held onto her long enough for her to regain her balance.

Embarrassment washed over her from head to toe.

"Oh, I'm so sorry, I'm just… clumsy… sometimes."

It was a lie. She had never been clumsy a day in her life. In fact, she could maneuver across a street without her feet ever touching the ground. She could scale a smooth wall using the tiniest grips and holes for support.

"You'd better be careful. The stones on these streets are so uneven."

She let out a nervous chuckle. "Yes, of course. I shall be more careful…"

He allowed her to compose herself and then stuck his elbow out so she could hold onto it with her hand again.

She smoothed the front of her dress with her other hand and continued their stroll.

"So?" he prodded. "Will you dine with us tomorrow?"

She knew she should say yes. This was the perfect opportunity to sneak around and retrieve the map… somehow.

She swallowed her doubts and fears and smiled at him with a confident gaze. "Yes, of course."

But her insides twisted like the braids woven together in the case beneath her bed.

The sooner you get this over with, the better, she told herself.

All the societal lessons about propriety and manners and ladylike behavior swirled in Zinnie's head.

"You can do this," she muttered under her breath.

Lela clicked her agreement.

Zinnie's lips twitched. She was too nervous for a full smile to stretch them all the way, but she appreciated Lela's encouragement.

She probably shouldn't have brought Lela to dinner. Feathers and food don't mix. That's why people don't keep pet birds in their homes where people may eat or drink or prepare food.

But her stomach was in knots, and she just couldn't bring herself to arrive at Atlas's house alone. She wore her hair half pulled up and braided, and the underside loose with curls cascading past her shoulders.

When he led her into the dining room where his family awaited her arrival, he didn't take his eyes off her. They glowed with admiration and the natural blush that darkened her cheeks probably only added to her beauty in the moment.

She, on the other hand, focused on the rich velvet curtains, the smooth hardwood floor, and the deep mahogany table laden with silver edged plates and shiny flatware. The plush rug beneath the table felt like thick moss beneath her feet. She imagined taking her shoes off and allowing the softness to squeeze between her toes. She had never felt moss between her toes before. It was one of the things on her list that she wished to experience when she finally escaped the city.

Soon, she reminded herself. *Very, very soon.*

As the servants served the first course, Atlas spoke to the family. And to Zinnie, of course.

"Father, Mother, I heard that the city puts on a huge festival to mark midsummer." He leaned toward them with bright eyes.

Gentlewoman Forster glanced at Zinnie. "Really?"

Zinnie did her best to add polite comments to the conversation, but her rattled nerves about the situation left her on edge.

"Um, yes." All the confidence that she usually exhibited floated out the window like a dandelion fluff on the breeze.

Lela stroked her neck with her soft feathers. The touch calmed her.

"It's quite the annual event. Everyone goes all out..."

What else should she say about it? It hadn't ever been anything special to Zinnie. She always had extra work during the festival.

She took another bite to occupy her mouth while she figured out the next thing to say.

What had come over her? She had participated in plenty of lessons on meal decorum and proper usage of the many utensils. But she found herself stumbling through the meal. Using the wrong fork or spoon, biting the fork too hard, or dribbling a little of her cider onto her plate.

Her practice in subtlety lent itself well to the situation, and she managed to cover up her fumbles before anyone noticed.

Lucy kept giving Zinnie sideways glances throughout the meal, which only added to Zinnie's nervousness. Did Atlas's sister suspect something? Was Zinnie giving away the fact that this was not how she actually lived her life, but was merely an act she performed for their sake?

When the family adjourned to the sitting room, Zinnie tried to make her escape. "Thank you for the lovely meal…"

Lucy, however, swooped in, hooked her arm through Zinnie's, and dragged her along behind her parents.

Zinnie didn't resist. That would only make the situation more suspicious.

Atlas noticed the interaction and laughed at his sister's antics. He made sure the ladies had comfortable seats and attended to their wishes for entertainment.

"Leave us alone for a moment, won't you, brother?" Lucy smiled sweetly at Atlas.

The hairs on the back of Zinnie's neck stood on end. Why did Lucy wish to speak with Zinnie privately? Was this the moment she had been dreading? Was her secret about to be exposed?

The serene expression on Lucy's face did nothing to indicate what she may ask. Or accuse.

Zinnie gulped. She steadied herself for whatever accusation Lucy may extend. Rehearsed in her head all the excuses she could make for her odd behavior this evening. For her sudden attention to Atlas. For her nerves and blushes.

Chapter 23

*T*hough her feelings for Atlas were true, she didn't think she could admit them out loud, especially not to his own sister.

She would say she had been unwell. That she hadn't slept well the previous night. That she had quarreled with her aunt before arriving for dinner.

Lucy leaned close and glanced around. She whispered, "Did you bring Lela to dinner?"

Zinnie stared. Her lips parted but no words emerged.

Lucy looked at Zinnie's face and raised her eyebrows. "I knew it! That's why you were acting so strange tonight. You didn't wish for my parents to find out, did you? I suppose bringing an animal to a meal would be seen as inappropriate. Did you bring her so I may see her again?"

Zinnie didn't move a muscle. She didn't really know what to think, let alone say.

Lela poked her head out from beneath

Zinnie's curls on her shoulder.

Lucy let out a quiet squeal. "I knew it! Oh, my *goodness,* she's so cute!" She gushed and stroked the soft feathers on Lela's head.

Lela cooed at the touch and fluffed her feathers.

Lucy giggled and slapped her hand over her mouth. She glanced at her parents to see if they had noticed, but they were deep in conversation with one another.

Zinnie allowed Lucy to fawn over Lela while she pricked her ears to try to hear what the adults had to say.

"We should play a card game. Felix," Atlas's mother addressed Gentleman Forster, "fetch the cards from the card table."

"No, no, Beatrice. Card games are too dull and do not allow for good conversation. A guessing game would be much more enjoyable." Gentleman Forster- Felix- answered.

Atlas noticed Zinnie's face pointed in their direction and stood to join her.

Zinnie motioned for Lucy to settle down and they both folded their hands politely in their laps.

Lucy gave her brother a charming smile. "Dear brother, how kind of you to join us. We were just having a lovely conversation."

"About Zinnie's pet dragon, right?" Atlas winked at Lucy and grinned at Zinnie. "I'm sure my parents would be delighted to meet Lela. I have mentioned her to them on occasion."

Zinnie's eyes went wide. "But…"

Atlas held up a hand to stop her. "I insist." He stretched a hand toward Zinnie.

She placed her own fingers in his outstretched hand. A spark ignited where their skin touched. By the look on Atlas's face, he had felt it, too.

Static from the carpet, she told herself, and allowed Atlas to help her rise from her soft chair.

"Mother, Father. Zinnie has something to show you." He did not let go of her hand as he led her the few steps across the room to join his parents.

Zinnie was at a loss for words. Again. She had never felt so out of sorts before. She didn't understand why she couldn't pull herself together.

And she kind of loved the way her tiny hand felt inside Atlas's large, warm one. She didn't want him to ever let go.

Beatrice Forster smiled warmly at Zinnie. Kindness shone from her the same as from Atlas.

"Oh… um…" Zinnie was tongue tied.

"Her name is Lela." Atlas brushed Zinnie's curls from her shoulder. His fingers grazed the skin on her neck. Warmth spread from the spot all the way up her neck and across her face.

Her hand that still rested in his tingled.

Lela emerged and climbed onto Atlas's hand. He released Zinnie's hand with his other one and stroked the dragon.

Her hand felt suddenly cold from the lack of connection.

Her breathing came faster. Her heart pounded. Her mind raced. How could she deceive this amazing family like this? It didn't matter that Jessamine had essentially threatened them, she shouldn't be doing this thing.

"It's alright, Zinnie. We don't mind having animals in the house," Felix insisted.

Atlas rested his hand on the small of Zinnie's back and gave her a questioning look. Her distress must have been plain to see.

She focused on his touch. On the warm smiles and kind gestures of all four members of this family. In that moment she decided to set aside what she had come here to do and try to just enjoy the evening. She would figure out a way to retrieve the map tomorrow. Besides, one more day of hair growth would only be a good thing for her imminent escape.

She still had thirteen days until the full moon. She had time.

She forced her breathing to slow in as subtle a manner as possible and put a smile on her own face to match theirs.

In no time, her heart slowed, her muscles relaxed. She found herself leaning into Atlas's touch. Joining the family in fawning over Lela. Relishing the dragon's antics. And even snorting with laughter when the tiny flame from the dragon's mouth accidentally lit Atlas's sleeve on fire. He tore off his overcoat and tossed it to the floor. He stomped on it several times until the flames went out.

Lela wore a self-satisfied expression on her face, though none of the others recognized it. She blinked her long lashes at Zinnie. Her eyes darted to Atlas.

Zinnie didn't understand why the dragon had done it at first, until the laughter died down and she realized that Atlas's arms from the elbows down were now bare. Her eyes followed his strong forearms to where his sleeves stretched across his muscular upper arms. The vest beneath his jacket matched his eyes perfectly. The whole look caused Zinnie's heart to flutter again.

She looked at her tiny friend and realized she had done it on purpose. She rolled her eyes but couldn't stop smiling.

The remainder of the evening was spent in laughter and games like "I Spy", where Zinnie bested each member of the family every time; sleight of hand tricks that impressed Atlas's family even more than she had expected; and stories from their travels that left Zinnie aching to hear more.

When the night grew late, Zinnie didn't want to leave. She *never* wanted to leave this home. This family, full of love and affection for not just one another, but their staff, and anyone whose path they may cross throughout their daily living.

She wished she had grown up like this, instead of always looking for a way to hide things, cheat people, and make a profit from anyone around her.

But she had no reason to stay in their home any longer. She allowed Atlas to escort her "home" again. When they stood face to face in front of "her" door, he leaned down and placed a gentle kiss on her cheek before turning and waving goodbye.

She rested a hand on the spot where his lips had touched her skin. Tears leaked from the corners of her eyes for the first time in a very long time.

It wasn't fair that he had to be so perfect. So kind and giving of himself. This all would have been easier if he had been selfish and arrogant like most of the men her age- of *any* age- in the city.

The short time she had known him he had challenged everything about her without even realizing it.

He didn't really know the real her, either.

Sure, she hadn't hidden her true personality from him- her cheerful attitude, lively conversations, and even some of her secret skills that no one besides Jessamine knew about.

But he didn't know her motives for spending time with him. He didn't know the truth about her past, her family, or her mistress. He didn't even know where she actually lived. If he chose to come call upon her here, he would be shocked to discover that the people who lived here knew nothing about her at all.

She needed to finish this mission before she lost her heart to him completely and risked losing him, too.

"I must steal it, Lela. Tonight. Then we leave." She said the words in a hushed tone as she watched his silhouette walk away from her. She couldn't afford to wait any longer.

Her eyes stung as she changed out of her evening dress and into her dark blouse, laced bodice, black trousers, and ankle boots.

She cut as much length from her hair as she could, leaving

a short boy-style haircut behind. She took the time to expertly weave all the locks hidden beneath her bed into one enormous length of rope. Not only did it prepare her for her escape, but it passed the time while she waited for the moon to rise and the city to quiet for the night.

With the dark cloak covering her entire body from head to toe, she blended with the middle of the night darkness.

She left Lela home, even though the dragon wanted to come for this venture. She couldn't risk anyone in Atlas's house recognizing the dragon.

Her throat tightened as she rehearsed the plan in her head on the way there.

Her heart ached as she snuck into the garden where she had shared a lovely picnic with Lucy and Atlas only eight days ago.

She knew where Felix's study was located in the house. *Not Felix. Gentleman Forster.* If she thought of him as a person, or as Atlas's father, she might change her mind. She must think of him only as a mark. Nothing more.

She knew just which pillar to climb, which window seal to break. She would need to search quietly once inside, for she did not know the exact location where he kept his most prized maps safe from harm or theft.

Theft.

The word struck her like errant lightning.

She squeezed her eyes shut and forced her bottom lip to stop quivering.

She would do this thing.

She would leave the map on Jessamine's table.

She would gather the rope woven from her own hair.

She would leave.

And never look back.

But she couldn't stop thinking of the image of Atlas's hurt face when he discovered that the woman he had been spending time with did not live at the house he had thought.

When his father discovered his map to be missing.

When the family would finally put the pieces together and discover that she had been false in her intentions.

She couldn't even leave him a note that explained it all, because there really wasn't a good explanation. Anything she said would not be believed. If only she could just talk to him one last time. Feel his eyes on her, her hand in his, his lips on her cheek.

Her cheeks burned.

She flexed her fingers and forced herself to get into the right mindset for the job that must be done.

She crossed the garden. Turned away from the place where she had laughed with her new friends.

Fake friends.

She climbed the pillar that would lead her to the second story window that housed the study.

She made it halfway up when a sudden noise below caused her to freeze in place.

Chapter 24

Her dark clothing kept her hidden in the shadows. No one would be able to see her.

But it wasn't a person that approached below.

It was a badgerdragon. It sniffed the ground where she had stepped moments before. It lifted its gaze and followed her path up the pillar.

Its glowing eyes locked right onto her exact location.

"No…" she breathed.

It let out an unnatural sounding screech as an alarm to alert the house of an intruder.

"No!" she growled. "*No!*"

Words like "failure" and "useless" buzzed around her head. She would not mention this turn of events to Jessamine when she asked for an update.

At least badgerdragon wings were too small for them to fly.

She shimmied up the pillar the rest of the way, leapt to a ledge that would be just a little too far for most people, and climbed up the third story wall of the house.

The animal below followed her path and continued to sound the alarm.

Movement from inside the house proved that the alarm had been effective.

She heard Gentleman Forster's voice as he opened a door on the ground floor and entered the garden. "Who's there?" He held his lantern high, but the light did not reach Zinnie's location.

She crouched and raced across the peak of the roof toward the corner near the front of the house.

One last look over her shoulder showed a pair of manservants join Felix in the garden to search for the intruder.

Zinnie picked up speed, leapt into a tree in front of the house, and slid down the trunk all in one fluid movement.

She disappeared into the shadows and zig zagged through the city to find her way home. She couldn't risk leaving a trail that led directly to where she slept, so she spent a good hour crisscrossing her own path, climbing gates, entering buildings and leaving by another way, before she finally slipped into her own room and collapsed on the bed in a heap of tears and exhaustion.

Lela peered at her from inside her cage. She pushed the door open and flew to Zinnie's side. The tears that dripped from the dragon's eyes burned and sizzled when they landed on Zinnie's skin, but the comfort of knowing she did not suffer alone drove the pain from her mind.

They weren't the rumored healing tears of some kind of pixie, but they helped her find sleep before her own tears could dry on her pillow.

"It's a job, Lela, just like all the other jobs I've ever done for her. And it's the very last one, too. Then we'll use my stash of hair to get out of here. Don't look at me like that."

Zinnie let out a sigh and dropped her hands to her sides from where they had been styling her hair for her meeting with Atlas that day. Fortunately, it had grown long enough overnight for her to do something presentable with. Adding a few flowers here and there covered up the difference in length from her usual style.

Lela didn't move from her perch.

"I know they are good people. That's why I must protect them by doing this job." She turned to fully face the dragon. "You understand that, right? You'll help me if I need it?"

Zinnie's eyes were all puffy and red from crying herself to sleep the night before, and the compassion from her tiny friend had diminished by morning until Zinnie felt like she was being judged by a tiny dragon.

She sighed and turned back to the mirror. "I'll just do it by myself if I have to. It's the only option." Her firm voice betrayed her conflicting emotions about the whole thing.

Lela left her perch and landed on Zinnie's arm. She fluffed her feathers and tipped her head to one side.

Zinnie relaxed her shoulders. "Thank you, Lela. I knew you'd be there for me. It's all going to work out, you'll see."

Lela clicked her teeth. She let out a growl.

"It will. It has to."

Zinnie put the finishing touches on her hair, turned back and forth to examine her reflection, and left the building to find Atlas before he tried to find her at her fake home.

She was so close to finishing the job she couldn't risk messing it up now. Especially knowing they had a badgerdragon guarding their house. There was no way to sneak in and steal it. She needed to procure another invitation, cause a distraction, slip away, and steal the map. Then everything would be fine. It *would* be fine.

It was a good thing she hurried because she did find Atlas headed in the direction where he had delivered Zinnie safely home the previous night. His whole face lit up when he saw her.

Lela swooped around the pair when Atlas extended his hand toward Zinnie.

Zinnie gladly accepted the offer of further contact.

"Good morning," she said, breathless from her quick pace.

His warm smile radiated his affection for her. "Good morning." He squeezed her hand.

"Where shall I show you today?" she asked in a pretend proper voice as if she was his guide and not his friend.

Lela, bored by the pair and busy with her own desires for a tasty insect snack, flew away from them.

"Wherever you like." He tucked a curl behind her ear and allowed his hand to linger on her cheek.

"I was thinking..." she started to say.

Atlas withdrew his hand in a flash and covered his mouth with his elbow. A wet cough shook his torso.

"Atlas, are you well?" Zinnie squeezed his hand and planted her worried eyes on his face.

He coughed again and patted his chest to clear his airway. "I'm fine, just a tickle in my throat."

She gave him a skeptical look.

He smiled and reassured her he was fine. "Lead the way, my beautiful Zinnie."

She let her worries about his health fade and focused on the task at hand. She must procure an invitation to his home. She must *not* get distracted by his charming behavior and good looks. She only had twelve days left.

The plan ran through her head. Again. Some of the details had changed since the discovery of the badgerdragon. Much was the same though: Enter the home. Get Atlas to show her the map. Present a distraction. Steal it. Deliver it to Jessamine.

She daydreamed about Atlas *giving* her the map. He seemed to enjoy her presence as much as she did his. Maybe if she was charming enough, he would just hand it over?

She told herself it was improbable, but it wasn't impossible.

When another cough racked his body a few moments later she stopped dead in her tracks. "Atlas, you are not well. That cough sounds severe. Have you fallen ill?"

He shook his head and gave her a sheepish expression. "I may have been exposed to the sweating sickness a few days ago, but I have felt fine until this morning. I'm sure it is nothing, just the dry air." He suppressed another cough.

"The sweating sickness is serious, Atlas. How did you become exposed?" Of course, she already knew the truth, but he didn't know that she had seen him there.

He recounted his visit to the boarding house where he had shared his family's bounty with those less fortunate.

"Why would you expose yourself like that? The risk is high for you and your family since you are new to the city." Zinnie's mouth turned down for probably the first time in his presence since they met.

He paused in his steps. He faced her and took her other hand in his, so he held both her hands now.

"Zinnie, it was worth the risk to serve those less fortunate."

"But what if something happens to you?" She choked on her words.

In the back of her mind, she was aware that it shouldn't really matter to her. Within the next few days, she would leave and never see him again. But she wanted to know that at least he was happy and safe. Or at the very least, safe.

"If you had seen the faces of those that I visited, you would have done the same thing for them as I." His eyes were full of compassion and concern for those he had visited.

And he was right. Zinnie had seen their faces. They looked at him with eyes full of joy and gratitude, as if they had been visited by a fabled healing Forest Prince instead of a mere human.

"*Atlas.*" His name fell from her lips with such tenderness that the sound of it made her eyes well with tears. "You are too good for this place." She released his hand and swiped at her eyes. "You do not belong here. It is a city filled with those who are selfish and deceitful. You should leave. Your whole family should leave before something tragic changes everything for you."

She wished she could say more, but she must keep her words cryptic.

He stepped closer to her and used his free hand to gently brush the tears from her cheek with his thumb.

She closed her eyes and savored the tender touch.

When she opened her eyes to look at him again his smile was warm.

"*You* are not selfish and deceitful, Zinnie. I have to believe there are more people in the city like you. And perhaps people like my family, like you, and I, can spread some goodness and light to others around us. We can be a light for them in this darkness." He looked around at their surroundings and met her eyes again.

A sob escaped her lips at his words.

Jessamine had only ever told her about her shortcomings. The woman had never paid Zinnie a single complement in her entire life. Everything she said was calculated and underhanded.

Atlas wrapped his arms around her and pulled her close. He cradled her head with one hand and held her back with his strong arm.

The embrace startled her. The contact more comforting than she could have imagined. How had she gone so long without this kind of affection? Maybe she would have turned out to be a very different person if she had been cared for like this.

The thought only made her feel worse. She cried into his chest, letting all of her vulnerabilities pour out of her, but keeping the truth firmly locked away inside her heart.

When he realized the truth about her, would the betrayal break him? Would he become cynical and hardened like everyone else in this place? Was she about to snuff out the little light that shone in this city of darkness?

He pulled back, wiped her tears with his thumbs and held her face in both his hands. "You'll see, Zinnie. I promise, we can make a difference. Together."

She could only nod. She had to protect him by any means necessary.

Another cough shook his lungs, but not as bad as the earlier ones. Maybe he would be alright from the sweating sickness.

"Come with my family to the festival tomorrow?" He studied her face and eyes for her answer. "Let's see how much light we can spread."

She nodded again.

He took her hand. "In the meantime, let's see the rest of this city and figure out where our light will be best utilized."

Chapter

25

Preparations had already begun for the midsummer festival that was to take place the following day. Families and lovers had collected flowers from without the city walls to decorate every door frame, windowsill, street pole, and awning. Woven garlands and wreaths hung on doors, carts, and around the necks of pack animals.

Winged insects and winged creatures of all kinds flocked to the flowers in abundance, attracted by their sweet scents and bright colors. They added even more color, movement, and ambiance to the festive atmosphere.

Vendors set up displays of various shaped and sized baskets.

Lela returned with a tiny ring of flowers hanging around her neck.

Atlas admired their delicate beauty, and quizzed Zinnie. "Traditionally people purchase baskets and bouquets to secretly leave to friends and neighbors, right?"

"Yes… and no," Zinnie said. "In other places they do. But… the people of Dorian do things a little differently…"

How could she tell him that everything that was done here had ulterior motives? People gave baskets to those they owed money or favors to, hoping to stay within their good graces. They used the flowers to bury messages of intrigue, secret payments, or even items to be used for blackmail. They tried to gain favor with the city leaders by camouflaging expensive gifts amongst the bouquets of flowers. Nothing was given or received without a specific reason.

"But… mostly yes." She kept those details to herself.

He would figure out the truth if they stayed in the city long enough. There was no need to spoil his ideas of what the holiday should represent.

They ate food reserved for the midsummer festival. Vendors always sold items early, to make more money, of course, instead of only selling on the festival day.

"Sweet breads are my favorites," Zinnie hummed as she took a bite of her pastry.

"I don't think I've seen you look as happy as you do right now!" Atlas laughed at the satisfied look on her face.

She grinned at him.

He brushed a crumb from her lip.

She blushed and thanked him.

"Would you like to try a bite?" She offered the pastry to Atlas.

"And deny you the pure joy that eating that pastry is bringing you? No way. I'll just watch." He folded his arms and grinned.

She shrugged and shoved the last couple of bites into her mouth. She licked the stickiness from her fingers. "I could eat that every day and never tire of it!"

"I believe it!" he laughed.

By evening, Zinnie's head and feet were tired. The lack of

sleep from the previous night's events, the crying that had kept her from resting well, and the battle of guilt and protection that raged in her head left her exhausted.

"You look like you're wilting." Atlas stroked her back.

Zinnie stifled a yawn. "I'm fine, really."

"I should take you home if you are to spend the entire day with me tomorrow."

She needed to get him to take her back to his home. But he was right. The day had grown too late for her to return home with him. His kindness had distracted her until she had lost complete track of the hour.

He led them toward her false-home and stopped in front of the door. For someone who was supposed to be highly observant, she sure let herself slip around him.

"What time shall I arrive to escort you?" He stood close in front of her and smiled while he waited for her to answer.

Zinnie hadn't thought about that detail. She couldn't have him show up here in the morning. "Oh, I'm an early riser. I'll meet you in front of your home."

He looked saddened, but he smiled and agreed.

"Goodnight." He squeezed her hand.

She waved and watched him bounce away from her.

She dragged herself back across town so she could go to bed for real. He was right. If she didn't get some rest, there was no way she would survive an entire day of celebrating and be able stay up for the late sunset and bonfires that were to follow. And the inevitable opportunity to finally steal the map.

She had never had this much trouble accomplishing a job before. And with the opportunity to leave the city that followed the completion of the theft for Jessamine, she couldn't understand why she allowed this to drag on for so long.

As she fell asleep, she had a fleeting thought that maybe

she was making it take a long time on purpose. Once the job was done, she would leave. Lose Atlas forever. And begin a brand-new life, all on her own. Maybe she was holding on to this dream of a future in Dorian that Atlas provided.

But she knew deep down it was nothing more than just a dream.

"If the city had looked festive yesterday, it looks like a completely different place today!" Zinnie breathed to Lela when she stepped outside the following morning.

She had performed her morning tasks in record time: dress, cut her hair, inform Jessamine of her plan to steal the map that day. She couldn't afford to be late.

Jessamine, of course, had commented on Zinnie's slow pace. "You sure are taking your time on this one, aren't you?"

Zinnie did her best to ignore the observation and hurried on her way.

Just like a hummingbird, Lela flitted to the various flower displays to suck on the variety of nectar.

They both admired the festival preparations as they made their way to meet up with Atlas and his family.

Every surface that could be lined, covered, or draped in flowers had been lined, covered, or draped in flowers.

Women and children wore halos of flowers on their heads liked crowns. Men wore boutonnieres of flowers on their jacket lapels.

Children ran around barefoot. Women wore light clothing with sleeves pinned up and hemlines held higher than usual by even more flowers.

The atmosphere could only be described as sunny.

If Zinnie hadn't lived in the city her entire life, she would have been deceived by the cheerfulness and goodwill that appeared to be spreading through the streets. She allowed herself to see things through the eyes of Atlas and his family for this day, and it turned the day into nothing short of magical.

She knew she had a job to do but was certain she could secure an invitation to their home by the end of the day. By this time tomorrow she would be out of the city and starting her new life.

The thought of leaving Atlas behind stung, but she knew it was for the best. He would never be able to love the woman she truly was. He only cared for the one he thought he knew.

Atlas's mother purchased a basket of blossoms for each of the five of them. Since they didn't know very many people, Zinnie showed them the poorer parts of town where the people would probably not be receiving any gifts from anyone that day. They would be busy earning a living by selling items instead.

They managed to leave each of the five baskets secretly on the doorsteps of five separate families that would appreciate the gesture.

Atlas was right. Spreading goodness and light left her feeling brighter than ever.

After a lunch of meat pies, spiced pastries, and candied nuts, the family- and Zinnie- settled on benches on one side of the main street to enjoy the parade. Lela curled up beneath Zinnie's hair for an afternoon snooze. Her soft feathers and regular breathing gave Zinnie a sense of peace in the midst of all the revelry.

Folk dancers performed to the music of traveling minstrels, acrobats and jugglers tumbled down the street and performed feats that even Zinnie found impressive, and children collected the hard-cooked sugar candies that the city leaders tossed from their decorated carriages as they waved at the crowds.

After the parade, Lucy and her parents decided to make their way toward the performance hall to watch a show, while

Atlas wanted Zinnie to show him where the less wealthy locals celebrated.

She took him to a market that visitors and the wealthy seldom visited. A minstrel performed a one-man show, telling tall tales about the giants coming down from the clouds to bring peace to the land. He told of secret springs of water that allowed someone to live forever.

"Can you imagine?" Atlas whispered in Zinnie's ear.

His breath tickled her neck, and she relished the feeling of his closeness.

"Living forever?" she whispered back.

"Yes! Imagine the amazing things you could see or do if you never had to worry about aging or anything. It would be a dream!"

Zinnie thought about it. Would she want to live forever? She supposed that depended on whether it was the life she lived at the moment, or the life she planned for herself once she escaped the city.

"What would you do with an unlimited number of lifetimes?" he asked her.

Her eyes went out of focus. She barely knew what she wanted to do when she left the city. "Explore," she breathed. "Meet new people, see new places…"

"Mmmm," he hummed. He moved a little closer beside her. "You could do so much good for so many people."

She stiffened. She had only been thinking about what she would do for herself. And here Atlas was, still thinking about what he could do for someone else.

"Are you alright?" he questioned with his arm around her shoulders.

She loved his touch but felt conflicted about his question. She wasn't alright. She was the furthest from alright than she had been for a long time. She never imagined having a friend, let alone a man that she had developed feelings for, when she planned to leave the city. It was always just her and Lela. And no one else.

She didn't quite know what to do with these new feelings. They rooted her to this place in a way she hadn't expected.

Yet, she knew she couldn't stay once she betrayed Atlas. He would never have her.

As long as she stayed, she would never be able to leave the life she currently lived.

Whatever grew between she and Atlas just wasn't meant to be.

She subconsciously pulled away from him, then remembered she still needed to play a part so she could get into his house and steal the map for Jessamine.

The cold, unfeeling eyes of her mistress loomed in her mind.

Time was running out.

Chapter 26

She put on a brave smile, leaned into his touch, which she truly didn't mind at all, and continued to try to enjoy these last happy moments before everything changed forever.

Today was the day to enjoy the sunshine, flowers, gift-giving, and the company by her side. She would think of nothing else until tomorrow.

After the minstrel finished his exaggerated history lesson, he played music for the people to dance to.

Atlas didn't know many of the folk dances, but the steps were rhythmic and easy to learn.

In no time the pair circled the street, linked arms with new partners, swung around, and returned to one another again and again.

Zinnie's hair swung behind her. Her face stretched with her smile. The breeze from the movements cooled her cheeks and neck. And the look on Atlas's face made everything worth it.

After the revelry they both agreed they needed to rest.

"How about your garden at home? It's so quiet and peaceful, away from the crowds?" Zinnie suggested while they walked hand in hand down the street at a slow pace to catch their breath.

Atlas squeezed her hand. "That sounds perfect." He tucked her hand in the crook of his arm, and rested his opposite hand over hers, interlacing their fingers.

Zinnie's stomach fluttered, and her mind spun. If he kept being so… wonderful… she might change her mind about leaving after all.

She remembered that she had secured her invitation to his home. The bonfires and further celebrations would pick up again after the late sunset, and the sounds and celebrations would be the perfect opportunity for her to find the map and hide it before he noticed anything.

They walked in comfortable silence. His words about spreading goodness to those in need kept replaying in her head. She wished she could have the life he lived. To be loved by parents and a sister, and even their servants! To have enough that you can share with others. To never wonder if your life had any value.

Her throat tightened. That's the kind of life she wanted for herself. She knew she wouldn't find it in Dorian, but perhaps there was a place like that for her somewhere across Tala. She only needed to find it.

Atlas interrupted Zinnie's introspection. "For you." His voice was thick, and his eyes brimmed with affection. He offered her a bouquet of zinnia flowers.

When had he purchased these? She must have been more caught up in her own thoughts than she realized.

Her breath caught in her throat. The jewel toned purples, reds, and oranges glowed in the afternoon sun. She took the bouquet from Atlas and buried her nose in the blooms sweet fragrance born from the perfumed water in which the florist stored them.

"Thank you," she breathed.

"There's a belief across Tala that if you place seven flowers beneath your pillow on midsummer's night you will dream of your future partner." His voice cracked a little on the last word. He studied her face for her reaction with a nervous smile.

She grabbed his arm and squeezed. She gazed up into his handsome face and her words came out heavy with emotion. "I hope I do dream of… him." She emphasized the last word and did not take her eyes from his.

His smile widened and he wrapped his arm around her waist. He held her close to his side as they continued their walk to his home, each relishing the presence of the other.

She pulled all the thoughts of her job and what it would mean for her heart and tossed them aside like weeds from a garden. Today, for right now, this thing she had with Atlas would be real.

Lucy joined them in the garden, and soon Beatrice did, too.

Lela entertained the other women with her aerial acrobatics and fire-breathing tricks.

"Where's Felix?" Zinnie asked.

She had a feeling she knew, but it was a good segue into talking about maps.

"He is in his study. Even on a celebration day he can't seem to leave those darn maps alone." Beatrice laughed at her husband's endearing fondness for maps.

"Has he been to all the places on the maps?" Zinnie asked next.

"Oh, no, but he has been to many of them," Beatrice answered. "He even sailed on a ship to the outer islands once before. He said the rocking of the boat made his stomach churn, but the sights and smells and sounds were all worth it." The pride that reflected in her eyes showed that she accepted the fact that he loved his family, but he also loved mapping their world, too.

"Maybe I'll make maps like that one day," Zinnie said without thinking.

She could see herself using her steady hand to draw all the details about her travels that most people wouldn't even notice. She could grow her skills and become a renowned cartographer herself.

"Do you have plans to travel?" Atlas asked.

She jumped a little and her eyes darted to his face. She had said that out loud? How was she going to explain this? "Yes, I would like to travel all of Tala one day…" Her voice was hushed. What would he think of her ambitious plans?

"I think that sounds tremendously adventurous!" Lucy piped in. "But I don't care for the traveling part so much myself!" She laughed at her own discomfort. "It can become rather dull after a while…"

"Lucy!" Atlas teased his sister. "Whatever do you mean? Are you saying now that I best you at 'I Spy' every time you no longer care to travel the world?"

Lucy pushed his shoulder and the two of them laughed together.

Lucy coughed, much like Atlas had done the day before.

Zinnie didn't like the startled expression on Atlas's face afterwards.

"Lucy, are you well?" Atlas inquired.

"I'm sure she's in good health, Atlas." His mother calmed her son. "You worry too much."

But Lucy coughed again. Harder this time. When she pulled her hand away from her face a look of horror pulled on her features.

She turned her hand to face the others. It was spattered with red droplets.

"Lucy!" Atlas jumped to his feet. "Mother, call the doctor. She has the sweating sickness. Come, Lucy, let's get you in bed."

"I really feel fine, Atlas," she insisted. Then her eyes sank closed, and she collapsed onto the ground.

At that moment Atlas screamed for assistance from the servants. Beatrice rushed to her daughter's side.

Pandemonium erupted all around Zinnie. She had no idea what she was supposed to do. Lela returned to Zinnie's shoulder and kneaded her shoulder with her claws.

The family was distraught over Lucy's sudden turn for the worse and had all but forgotten she was even present.

Zinnie stayed still, backed up, and slowly stood. Her hands twisted together in front of her. Now would be the perfect time to take the map. No one would even notice.

She could leave Lela as a lookout. Enter the study. Find the right map, stash it in her skirts, and leave before anyone even realized she was missing. It's what Jessamine would expect. It's what she would have done a few weeks ago.

But she couldn't bring herself to take advantage of the family's sudden tragedy in that way.

"I'll just come back… later," she whispered to no one.

She snuck out the front door of the house. Something she never thought she would do before. It was always a window or side door or servant's entrance.

She looked back at the home over her shoulder and could still hear the panicked voices coming from inside. A servant rushed past her, nearly knocking her over, as he ran for a physician to come treat the girl.

Zinnie walked through the streets as if in a stupor.

"Oh, Lela. What if Lucy doesn't recover before the full

moon? Would Jessamine have mercy on the fact the family is ill?"

She knew the answer. No. Jessamine would expect Zinnie to take advantage of the situation to procure the map. Fewer potential alarms and repercussions.

She would not tell her mistress of this turn of events. She would just watch carefully and hope that Lucy would recover in time for Zinnie to spend time with the family again.

It was a shallow hope, but she held onto it with everything she had.

When she arrived at her room, she noticed that the bouquet of zinnia flowers dangled from one hand. She had been so caught up in the events that she hadn't even remembered scooping them off the ground back at Atlas's house and carrying them all the way home.

She breathed in their scent and closed her eyes. Her heart cracked for the way her life had changed over the past few weeks.

She didn't believe in the stories about dreams that show your future, but if she had any chance of dreaming about Atlas's beautiful face and even more beautiful character, then she would stop at nothing to dream it.

She carefully placed the seven zinnia blossoms beneath her pillow and fell asleep without even thinking about cleaning up or changing her clothing. Or cutting her hair.

The tower loomed in front of her; its top stretched to the clouds. A hand gripped her wrist and tugged her toward the hidden door at the base of the tower. She followed the arm to a muscular shoulder and a tanned, handsome face. She recognized the sharp features and kind steel eyes.

"Atlas? What are you doing?"

"It's the least you deserve after the way you have betrayed me and my family. To think that it's your fault Lucy is sick. If anything else happens, you shall remain here for the rest of your life."

Zinnie's eyes grew into wide circles. "Atlas?" she whispered.

"You lied to me, Zinnie. Now go. I never want to see your face again."

He shoved her through the door and slammed it behind her.

The darkness surrounded her. She couldn't see her hand in front of her face. She frantically searched for a handle or hinges or any way to flee the darkness.

The door vanished. There would be no escape.

She sank to the floor and buried her head in her arms.

"What have I done?"

She woke up with tears streaming down her face and soaking her pillow. Even Lela's hot tears and soothing feathers did nothing to ease the pain.

Her heart felt as though it would crack.

But the memory of Jessamine's dark eyes reminded her that she must continue with the plan.

Lucy's illness was not her fault.

She would keep going. Wait for the family to heal. Then she would find a way to take the map.

She groaned. This had already taken too long. She had allowed Atlas to steal her heart.

She scoffed at the thought. *She* was the thief. And yet, he had stolen the thing most valuable to her. It was no less than she deserved.

A stem of green poked from beneath her pillow. She pushed the corner of her pillow aside. The now-squished zinnia flowers rested beneath her pillow. The memory returned of Atlas's words about dreaming of your future partner.

Would that dream become her future?

Chapter 27

Even though she had only known Atlas for a short time, Atlas's appearance still caught Zinnie off guard when she arrived at his home to check on Lucy with a fresh baked loaf of bread for his family. She had left Lela at home, not wanting to impose on the family by bringing her pet. She could have used her friend's comfort, though.

Atlas had dark circles beneath his blood shot eyes. His hair stood at funny angles from how often he ran his fingers through the strands. His normally warm toned skin looked gray and dim.

"I am glad to see you, Zinnie, but I don't have much time to visit today." He looked truly disappointed but sent a worried glance up the stairs toward his sister's bedroom.

"How… how is Lucy?" She was afraid to ask.

He pinched his lips and shook his head.

"Not well." He sighed and ran his fingers through his hair again.

"Atlas, you must get some rest…" She extended her hand to touch his arm. Before she could make contact, he stepped away and paced in front of her.

"I know. But I worry so much about her. What if the worst were to happen?" He froze in place and planted his stormy eyes on her. "I'll see you tomorrow. Hopefully by then she will be better."

He leaned forward as if to place a kiss on her cheek, seemed to think better of it, and turned on his heels to ascend the stairs.

Did he hesitate because he didn't want to risk Zinnie becoming sick? She had already been exposed, but Jessamine had access to cures that most others didn't know about. She had recovered quickly and had no long-lasting effects from the sweating sickness.

Or perhaps he hesitated because he realized that he didn't truly care for Zinnie as much as he had previously thought. When life takes a turn for the worst, it helps people see what's really important. In the big picture of Atlas's life, Zinnie was not all that important.

She guarded her heart against disappointment and rejection and hurried away from his home.

The temptation to climb below the city and flee at once tugged on her, but she had to finish this assignment from Jessamine. She just couldn't leave them like this. As if the inner conflict hadn't already been bad enough before, now the circumstance had become even more extreme. Her nerves remained on edge, worry clouded her thoughts. She slept terribly and went through the motions of her day in a haze.

When she returned to the Forster's mansion the following day, she was disturbed to learn that Atlas had succumbed to the sickness as well. The servant dismissed her before she could ask any further questions or ask to speak with his mother or father.

Even though she had been frustrated and disappointed by the dismissal, she had ways of finding out what she wanted to know on her own.

After the sun set, she donned her dark pants and cloak and climbed the exterior of his home. She cracked his bedroom window, slipped inside, and stayed in the shadows, just in case.

His steady, raspy breath proved that he was sound asleep, and she crept across the floor. Hopefully none of the floorboards would creak beneath her feet.

A lantern glowed dimly in the corner of the room.

His bedroom door stood tightly closed. Probably to reduce the risk of spreading the sickness to the rest of the family and staff that may not have already been exposed or fought off the infection themselves.

When she reached the edge of his bed, she stood very still and listened. The house was quiet. She lowered herself to the low bench beside the bed.

Would he sense her presence and awake? Would he recognize her through his fevered state? How would she explain her presence? Or her clothing?

Without thinking, she gently brushed a lock of his hair from his sweaty forehead. The heat radiated from his skin even though she didn't make contact.

"Oh, Atlas…" she sighed, barely above a whisper.

He didn't move or flinch.

"You shouldn't have given so much of yourself for everyone else. Even your sister. You should have been more careful. I don't know what I'll do if anything should happen to you…" Her voice caught in her throat. She couldn't believe she spoke the words out loud. Though she wished more than anything that he would wake up and be healed, she also hoped he would not wake while she spoke these words of the heart.

Tears ran in silent streams down her cheeks. She couldn't believe how freeing it was to say those to his face, even if he had no idea she was in his presence.

She caressed his forehead again and ran her hand down his cheek. The contact sent a wave of comfort through her skin. A feeling of home.

A silent sob escaped her lips. She sucked in a sharp breath when the floorboards in the hall moaned, and quiet footsteps edged closer to Atlas's room.

She hurried away from his bed and slid out the window. She stood on the ledge out of sight and peeked through the curtains.

His mother filled the place where Zinnie had just sat. She stroked his face and hands. Kissed his burning forehead. And closed her eyes to plead for him to come through this illness unscathed.

But Zinnie knew the truth. Once someone had succumbed to the fever in this manner, recovery was unlikely.

She also knew another truth. There was a way.

It would be risky, but she would do it.

For love.

For Atlas.

Another length of braids in the case beneath Zinnie's bed counted down to the day of her escape to freedom.

A modified visiting outfit allowed her to blend in with the members of high society.

A vial of syrupy liquid, removed from Jessamine's shop, weighed heavy in her pocket.

"If Jessamine ever found out that I've stolen from the shop…" she murmured to Lela as she prepared to run her very secret errand. "My nightmares of being locked in the tower will be the least of our concerns."

But she had to do something to save Atlas. She couldn't let either him or Lucy suffer any longer when there was a solution.

It took some convincing for Atlas's mother to believe that Zinnie had a cure for the sickness.

"I assure you; it is perfectly safe. I have taken it myself and I was healed in less than a day." Zinnie kept her voice calm but had a hard time hiding her strong emotions from the woman. Tears stung her eyes. She pushed through the tightness in her throat and forced her agitation for Atlas's safety to remain controlled.

Beatrice turned the vial over in her hands. She held it up to the light to observe the golden liquid that glowed in the cloudy daylight.

"What is in it? How does it work?" It was obvious she didn't *not* trust Zinnie, but she also would protect her children from something that she did not know anything about.

"It's made from the petals of the rampion flower." Zinnie kept out the part about the pixie magic that had been imbued in the mixture that gave it its true potency. "It has healing properties and has been found to be the perfect treatment for this type of ailment."

Beatrice did not say anything. Her own eyes were bloodshot and her face gray. It was likely she would come down with the sweating sickness as bad as her children. Worse, perhaps, because of her age.

Zinnie took a step closer. She covered the woman's hand that covered the bottle. She waited for his mother to look her in the eye. No deception crossed her mind or features or words when she begged, "Please, Beatrice, it will save him. Them." She changed the last word of her sentence quickly.

A glimmer in the woman's eye proved she had noticed the slip up. "You care for him, don't you?"

The tears Zinnie had been holding back broke through her emotional barrier. She could only nod in response.

"Very well. Come with me." She grabbed Zinnie's hand and dragged her up the stairs to Atlas's room.

She looked down the hall in either direction to make sure no one would accidentally witness what they were about to do. She shut the door and leaned her back against it. Her head rested against the wood, and she closed her eyes. Her mouth moved as if she spoke to herself, then she opened her eyes and hurried to Atlas's side.

"Just a few drops…" Zinnie instructed.

Beatrice removed the cork from the bottle and dripped the solution into her son's mouth.

She stared. "How long will it take?" she whispered without taking her eyes off her son.

"A day, no more." Zinnie wrung her hands together.

"Very well. You stay here. I will attend to Lucy." She turned away from Atlas. "I trust you, Zinnie. Don't make me regret it."

Guilt almost made Zinnie confess everything to Atlas's mother right then and there, but the woman left before Zinnie could even decide.

She collapsed beside Atlas's bed and buried her face in her hands. Her shoulders shook and the tears leaked down her arms to disappear into her sleeves.

"Oh, Beatrice, if you only knew. *Oh, Atlas, if you only knew.* You would not have given so freely of yourself to me. I do not deserve your family's kindness. You deserve so much more."

She allowed her sobs to subside and her tears to slow. She gingerly took his hand. The fever still wracked his body, but she knew he would survive the sweating sickness now.

This was her only chance to tell him how she truly felt,

without risking anything.

"You've taught me so much about life, Atlas. You've shown me selflessness. Strength. Courage. Compassion. I didn't know such kind, honest people even existed in the world until you came along."

Her thumb caressed his knuckles. The feeling of home returned. She rested her other hand on top of his so that she held him with both hands. She wanted to squeeze. To never let go. But she did not want to disturb his sleep. She must allow him to fight the sickness and heal.

"You've shown me how to trust for the first time. To realize how my actions truly affect other people. I won't burden you with everything, Atlas. But just know that what I will have to do, I do because I care about something for the first time in my life. Something other than my own situation."

He moaned and turned his head slightly.

She sucked in a sharp breath.

She didn't think she could risk him waking to find her there. It would be obvious she had been crying. She wasn't ready for him to really know how she felt. Not yet. Maybe not ever.

She slipped her hands away from him, pulled the door open, and turned to gaze upon his form on the bed. She took in his handsome features. Even when he was on his death bed, his features radiated kindness and strength.

He would be fine. From the sickness.

But she didn't know what would happen when he eventually found out the truth about her.

She snuck out of the house and ran away before she could change her mind. Before she chose him instead of Jessamine and the map. Before she spoiled everything for everyone.

Another restless night ushered in the new day. The day

when she would discover if the medicine worked. If Atlas and Lucy had survived the sweating sickness.

She would have to decide if she would steal the map. If she would escape the city. Or if she would throw all caution to the wind like dandelion puff pixies and make an entirely different choice altogether.

Her stomach twisted. Her back ached. Her eyes felt dry and puffy. She had barely slept. When her eyes closed, she saw either Atlas's funeral, or his look of betrayal when he discovered the truth about Zinnie. Either outcome left Zinnie gasping for air.

After another mild berating from Jessamine about her lack of appreciation for the kindness that Jessamine had extended her entire life, and questions about why this current job was taking Zinnie so long, Zinnie felt more defeated than ever.

She hurried through her morning errands while Lela remained hidden beneath her braids.

She changed into her clothing of high society to check on Atlas's family later in the afternoon, leaving Lela at home.

The city was alive with activity. Again. As if Zinnie's whole world wasn't on the brink of destruction.

The midsummer floating lights would take place that night. Zinnie had forgotten all about it until overhearing the excitement of the people around her.

Still, as much as she loved the once in a decade celestial display, she could only focus on Atlas.

And the map, she reminded herself. *Still the map. Don't forget the map!*

New tension pulled on her shoulders and weighed down her heart. If Atlas and Lucy had recovered, like she hoped, then she still needed a way to steal the map without being overcome with guilt. Or slipping up and getting caught. She had no intention of seeing the look on Atlas's face when he learned the truth about her motives. Or the motives that she had begun with. Her reasons for approaching the house today were vastly different than the first time.

"You can do this, Zinnie. You are a strong bloom. You have withstood worse. One step at a time. One day at a time. You still have time."

She swallowed the lump in her throat, forced her posture to straighten, and rapped her knuckles on the door. She braced herself for whatever fate would greet her on the other side.

Chapter 28

"Are you sure this is a good idea? What if we get caught?" Atlas's breathy voice called up to Zinnie from below.

Zinnie placed another hand above her head and pushed herself up the uneven stone wall with her opposite foot.

Lela taunted the pair from high above their heads.

"You have wings, Lela, it's no contest," she said to the dragon.

She turned her attntion back to Atlas. "You said you wanted the best view for the lights!"

Her heart felt as light as a hummingbird dragon as she scaled the tower wall. All urgency for leaving the city or stealing the map had vanished when Atlas greeted her with a healthy smile and warm embrace at his house earlier. The memory increased her joy more than she thought possible.

"I guarantee you this will be the best view."

"I'm not afraid of the height, or the climb." Atlas's voice came from a bit closer this time as he caught up to Zinnie so he could speak in a lower tone. "I am truly only concerned about whether we have permission to be here. And what might happen to us if we get caught."

Zinnie paused her ascent and looked over her shoulder at him. The brightness in his eyes, even against the darkness of the city below, lifted her spirits even more.

He had been on his death bed, and now he had the stamina to scale the tallest tower with her in the middle of the night.

She renewed her climb. "It will be fine. Don't worry! It's too dark to see since everyone has put out their lights tonight. And with our dark cloaks we will blend in with our surroundings if need be."

"I'll take your word for it." Atlas gave Zinnie a little boost as she climbed over the top of the tower. She lay on her stomach and reached for his hand. He waved away her assist and breached the top on his own.

"Are you sure you're not afraid of heights?" Zinnie teased.

He didn't look concerned at all about leaning over the edge to peer down the way they had come. "Not in the slightest." He gave Zinnie a curious look. "But I have to ask, how does a dignified young woman like yourself know how to do this?" He raised one eyebrow at her and smirked.

"Maybe I'm not as dignified as you thought." She pinched his arm and removed her cloak against the warm summer night air.

Atlas copied her and arranged the cloaks on the flat roof of the tower for them to recline upon.

Before they settled to gaze at the stars, though, Atlas leaned over the outside edge of the tower. "You can see all the way across the Dorian Sea from here! You're right, there is no better view in the city." He breathed in the clean air and his eyes drank in everything beyond the city.

The starlight danced on the surface of the sea. Zinnie couldn't wait for him to see what would happen when the midsummer lights appeared. He had no idea the surprise he was in for!

Lela disappeared over the wall and swooped to the beach below.

"Will she come back?" Atlas sounded worried for Zinnie's sake.

Zinnie smiled. "Always."

Atlas reclined with his back against one of the low battlement walls that created a semi-barrier around the perimeter of the circle. He motioned for Zinnie to sit on her cloak, too. She settled against the battlement next to him, which left more of a gap between them than she would have liked.

Before she could do or say anything about the distance, or tease him about heights, or even marvel at his miraculous recovery, Atlas cleared his throat.

"I don't know how to thank you, Zinnie. For saving Lucy's life and my own. We… I… will be eternally grateful for your quick thinking and knowledge of what to do. My mother never would have known, and for some reason the physician she called did not know of that treatment either."

Zinnie avoided eye contact. Of course, the physician wouldn't know, since it was a concoction of Jessamine's own making. She had used it to bribe people and blackmail them when the leaders became ill and needed a quick cure. At least Zinnie had been able to use it for someone that truly deserved it.

When she looked at Atlas again, his gaze hadn't left her face. She felt the heat climb her neck and spread across her cheeks. Fortunately, the midsummer lights hadn't arrived yet and the area was still dark.

He made sure she had locked eyes with him again. "I mean it. I owe you everything." His voice trembled.

She swallowed. "I am so glad you are well. And Lucy, too, of course," she hurried to add. "But…" she hesitated. She wanted to scold him for nearly killing himself in the service of others, but how does someone tell another that they are being too kind and giving? Was that even a real thing?

"But…?" Atlas encouraged her to continue. "Please be open with me. I feel as though you are a long-time friend. A companion. One I can trust wholeheartedly. Be honest with me."

"It's just… you should be more careful."

He chuckled. "Says the girl who climbs the highest towers in her free time."

She grinned and shrugged. "I guess I'm not just a regular girl."

"No, Zinnie. You are not just a regular girl." His voice was thick with emotion.

A heavy silence hung between them. One filled with anticipation and nerves.

Atlas broke the silence. "You were about to rebuke me for not being careful…"

She didn't quite know what to say. She decided, for once, to settle with the truth. "I was so scared, Atlas." She lowered her gaze to her twisting hands in her lap. "You give so much of yourself for everyone else. For your family. But at the expense of your own safety. I…" She choked on her words. "I don't know what I would have done if the worse should have happened." The last words came out as a whisper.

The warmth of him moving closer to her caused her to lift her gaze. He covered her hands with one of his and gently caressed the side of her face. His smile was warm and sincere. "I feel the same about you."

She nodded as tears filled her eyes and blurred her vision. "Then promise you won't risk yourself like that again?"

His shoulders slumped and it was his turn to lower his gaze.

"What is it, Atlas? Have I offended you?" She held her breath while she waited for his response.

"No, Zinnie. You could never do anything to offend me."

A voice in the back of her mind said, "That's what you think," but Zinnie pushed it aside and focused on the moment. She would worry about the rest tomorrow.

Atlas's soft voice spoke again. "I would like to confide in you something that no one knows. Not even my parents I don't think." He heaved a deep sigh.

She squeezed his hand with one of her own to encourage him to continue. To send the message that he could trust her, even though the truth was that no one could trust Zinnie as long as she worked for Jessamine.

A stab in her heart jolted her on the inside at the thought, but she didn't let the reaction show on the outside.

He squeezed his eyes shut and used his free hand to run his fingers through his hair, a trait that made her heart leap for a different reason.

"I was almost responsible for Lucy's demise once before. When we were younger. And I promised I would do anything, even give my own life, to prevent that from ever happening again." His voice cracked and he wiped a tear from sliding down his cheek.

"Atlas," Zinnie whispered his name, full of compassion and heartache for the man before her. "I'm sure whatever happened wasn't your fault..."

Atlas held up a hand to stop her. "I dared her to ride Father's new unbroken horse. She fell and hit her head. I almost could not awaken her. She didn't remember anything afterwards and I never told my parents.

"If my parents, or even Lucy, ever found out what I did, they would be appalled. Perhaps even wish to disown me."

Zinnie sighed. "Atlas, we all make mistakes. We all have secrets…"

He met her gaze again. "What are your secrets, Zinnie? What is one thing that no one knows about you?"

Her eyes widened. Did he know? Had he discovered the truth about her and was manipulating her to tell him once and for all?

He rushed to add, "You don't have to tell me anything, Zinnie. I would not force you to share your secrets with me. I feel as though we have a connection that I cannot deny. I feel close to you. Please don't feel pressured to tell me anything. I would be happy just to have you by my side for the midsummer lights. That's all I want from you tonight. I promise."

His sincerity cut to her core. He was the most honest person she'd ever met. She couldn't tell him the whole truth, but she could tell him something that almost no one in Tala knew about her.

She took a deep breath, smiled at him, and said, "I have special hair…"

He gave her a quizzical look and grinned. "You have… special hair?"

She laughed at her own discomfort and the tension between them dropped in an instant. "It's really hard to explain, and I don't even know the whole story behind it, but I have special hair."

He stroked the long braid that hung over her shoulder. "It is soft. And the color is brighter than almost anyone I've seen before. But… special? How so?"

"Alright, just hear me out. My hair grows extremely fast."

"And…?"

"Atlas. Not like, cut it twice a month fast, or even once a week fast. I cut my hair *every day*. If I don't, it will grow to the ground in twenty-four hours. I once let it grow for a week when I was young, and it stretched to ten times my current height behind me."

He squinted his eyes and tugged on her braid. "Are you playing with me? Your hair grows that fast?"

"Like I said, it's strange, I know, but it's true."

"How come I've never noticed?"

"I can hide the change well with the right kind of hair style. And I carry pins and ribbons with me to fix it up throughout the day. To be honest, I've never spent enough time with one person that I've needed to worry too much about anyone noticing. That is, not until I met you."

Atlas leaned closer to Zinnie. He laced his fingers between hers with one hand and ran his other down her hair from her scalp to the bottom of the braid.

Bunnyflies exploded in her stomach. She was at a total loss for words.

His eyes flicked to her lips.

Just as he moved closer to make contact, the first of the midsummer lights illuminated the sky like a mirrored spotlight shining on the city.

They both craned their necks to the sky to get a better view.

"This *is* the best view in the city!" Atlas pulled Zinnie to his side so she could lean on him as he leaned against the side of the tower.

"Just wait, Atlas, the real show hasn't even begun."

Chapter 29

Zinnie didn't know which view was better: the midsummer lights, or Atlas's expression at seeing them in the City of Dorian for the first time.

Slow-moving stars paraded across the sky from one horizon to the other. Sparks streamed behind them. Some shot out faster than the main bodies.

"They're different colors!" Atlas exclaimed and pointed at the sky.

Violet, pink, yellow, and red fragments sparkled against the blanket of darkness above.

The procession continued until the entire sky lit up with the stately celestial display.

"Atlas," Zinnie murmured. "Look down." She pulled him to stand beside her on the outermost part of the wall.

He sucked in a deep breath. "It's… spectacular!"

The parade of lights in the sky was a work of wonder, but what made this vantage point special for Zinnie was the remarkable display reflecting on the still waters of the Dorian Sea.

As the sparks floated to land on the water, luminescent creatures from below surfaced to greet them.

Glowing tentacles, fish, and naiads breeched the surface. The fish-like women reached their hands skyward to catch the sparks in their fingers. The entire sea alighted with brightness from above and below.

"I've never seen anything like this. I've seen the lights before, of course, when I was young, but we didn't live anywhere near the sea." Atlas's eyes bounced from the sky to the sea and back again.

"There's even more." Zinnie had never smiled so much in her life. Experiencing this display by herself for the first time had been memorable. Sharing this with Atlas would be unforgettable.

She watched his eyes reflect the lights and they grew impossibly wider.

His jaw dropped. "No, way…" he whispered.

She followed his gaze.

Sure enough, just as she expected, every glowing insect, creature, and flower in and around Dorian lit up. The brightness rivaled the morning sunrise, with a rainbow of colors. The creatures not bound by water below floated upward to dance with the lights in the sky. They surrounded Atlas and Zinnie.

Atlas leaned close to Zinnie. "I feel as though I am floating right alongside them all. Like I could reach up and touch the midsummer lights with my fingertips…" Laughter that reflected pure joy erupted from Atlas's lips.

"Look at them all!" He whirled around and pulled Zinnie close to his side. He wrapped an arm around her waist and held her close.

They both extended their hands toward the sky. Laughter bubbled out from both of them, and Zinnie couldn't stop smiling from ear to ear.

Atlas squeezed her closer. "Thank you so much for bringing me here. This would definitely not have been the same from below. Why doesn't everyone climb to the tower tops to watch the lights over the sea? Why would they want to miss this?"

Zinnie shook her head. She had wondered the same thing when the lights appeared ten years ago. She climbed to the tower many nights during the summer to gaze out across the sea. To daydream about a life of freedom. So, when she saw the display from the lights the last time they appeared, she had been baffled by the beauty. And by the fact that no one else seemed to notice. Or else they just didn't appreciate the beauty of the world around them.

"I think everyone is too busy focused on their own problems, or their own desires, to care about the wider picture. Tala has many wonderous things to offer, if people would just go look. At least, that's what I've heard..."

Zinnie stopped herself before she divulged more about her life and who she really was. If she confided about her captivity, he would want to know more. He would discover that she worked for Jessamine and that she wasn't just a society girl stuck with boring caretakers that never took her out on an adventure.

Atlas didn't appear to notice her inner struggle, or her slip of the tongue. He only had eyes for Zinnie. They swam with emotion as he caressed her face with his gaze.

How was she not supposed to fall in love when he looked at her like that? Her heart swelled, and she pushed all thoughts of her reality away so she could enjoy this moment.

She would probably never have another one like it. In fact, she was sure of it.

In ten years, she would be far away from this place. Atlas would be a distant memory. She would be on her own...

"I must confess, Zinnie, that you have stolen my heart." His husky words brought her back to the moment.

The irony of his statement did not escape Zinnie's conscience. But his next words surprised her even more.

He cupped her face with one hand. His eyes were moist. "I heard what you said to me while I was sick." He choked on his words.

He had heard? How much? Which time? Why hadn't he responded or said anything until now?

He continued before she could voice any of her thoughts. "I am sorry you have lived a life where you haven't been able to trust those around you. Or have known people who put others needs before their own. Where I come from those are common traits. But I see now that the City of Dorian is a different place than we imagined. I don't know if I have so much strength or courage as you seemed to see in me, but my heart is full of compassion for those around me. Including you."

Swirled among his words in her head was the thought that it was a good thing she didn't say more about her life or her mission.

Atlas continued. "But that's not why I like you so much, Zinnie. You have taught me things that I didn't even know I needed to learn. I do tend to bear the weight of the world on my shoulders too often. I do need to allow myself to be selfish once in a while. To loosen up and have fun.

"Sometimes I feel as though I will crack under the pressure I put on myself. But you have taught me to see things in a different light. To see the beauty in the world all around me."

He gestured toward the lights over the sea.

"To appreciate the little things right in front of me."

He pointed at the burning fireflies floating around them.

"To allow my *own desires* to come first sometimes."

He pinned his eyes back onto her face, emphasizing the

word *desire* when he looked at her.

He let out a warm laugh. "Besides the other things I didn't even know that I didn't know, like sleight of hand, and the ability to not be so proper all the time."

He gestured at their vantage point. "I never would have thought to climb the tower to see this. And look at what I would have missed!"

He stopped talking and caressed her face with his thumb.

She hadn't realized that tears had leaked from her eyes. He wiped them away with both hands and leaned his forehead against hers.

She breathed in his sun-kissed scent and closed her eyes.

The tender kiss he placed on her lips filled her with a warmth she had never known before.

It deepened the crack forming in her heart.

She allowed herself to kiss him back. To enjoy this moment before she would end up shattering his heart, too.

Chapter 30

You seem to have been enjoying your time with this *Atlas* boy and his family."

Jessamine's voice was filled with suspicion and impatience.

Lela shuddered beneath Zinnie's hair, out of sight but still very much aware of Jessamine's presence.

Zinnie paused mid-bite of her morning porridge. She swallowed the sticky lump already in her mouth and nodded. "It's for the job, of course Mistress Jessamine."

Jessamine gave her a knowing look and returned to her own meal. "I'm sure, Little Flower."

Zinnie didn't like the way the fake endearment sounded on Jessamine's lips.

"And why have you not been able to retrieve the map for me yet? If you are only focused on the job. It seems you would have it by now. I know your skills. I know of what you are capable…"

Zinnie rested her spoon in her bowl and pushed it away from

her just the slightest. Her appetite had disappeared.

All the warm feelings she had been carrying since she returned home just before dawn dissipated in that moment. She had already anticipated this conversation. The truth was, she had no good excuse. But she was sure she could convince Jessamine otherwise. She was decent at deceit after all…

She steadied her heart and her voice and clenched her hands in her lap beneath the table so Jessamine wouldn't see her white knuckles and shaking fingers.

"His father did not bring all of his maps with him. He is awaiting final arrival of their belongings any day now."

"I see." Jessamine pretended to eat her porridge, but she didn't actually bite her food and swallow it as usual.

Zinnie's heart plummeted into the bottom of her stomach. Had Jessamine slipped something into Zinnie's food? The woman had ways of controlling people, forcing them to tell the truth, even changing them to be what the woman wanted them to be.

But she wouldn't do that to Zinnie, right? Her mistress trusted her… didn't she? Zinnie was glad she had stopped eating, just in case.

"Have you… I don't know, tried *asking* the son about the maps?"

Zinnie smiled and tipped her head to the side in a display of youthful innocence. "I did at first, but Atlas isn't all that interested in them. If I bring it up too much, he might grow suspicious."

"And what *is* this boy interested in?" Jessamine sipped her morning tea.

Thoughts flashed through Zinnie's mind. He loved serving others. He loved the outdoors. He loved to travel, to read, and to learn.

"He enjoys studying laws. He wishes for a position in the government." This statement couldn't be further from the truth, but she wanted to protect Atlas from Jessamine, even in the smallest way.

"You have done your assignment of learning about your mark well. I hope you haven't done it *too* well and grown too fond of his handsome face." Jessamine looked at her straight on now as if she could see into Zinnie's soul and read her darkest secrets.

It wouldn't surprise her if she had a way to do that, too, but Zinnie had learned long ago to guard her thoughts and secrets carefully around most people. She only thought of the lights that had floated in the sky last night and tuned out all memories of Atlas.

"I am doing just what you asked, Mistress." She dipped her head in a subservient manner.

"Good. You do realize, however, that the full moon is only a week away. You are running out of time." Jessamine stood suddenly and carried her dishes to the wash basin in the corner. "I hope you are prepared for the consequences if you fail to comply with my request before then."

Zinnie didn't like how Jessamine used the words "comply" and "request", as if she had a choice in the matter at all. And she didn't like being reminded of the ticking clock, either.

"I believe there will be another celebration before then, *Flower Blossom*. Perhaps you will find a way to obtain my treasure then?" Jessamine kept her back turned to Zinnie, but Zinnie noticed the woman's ear turned in her direction. She was paying close attention to Zinnie's reaction.

"Yes, Atlas did mention something of the sort. I am concerned about his family. If they catch me in the act..."

"A disguise would serve you well." Jessamine sounded like she was clenching her jaw. Her patience truly was growing thin on this.

Zinnie sat up a little straighter. She really gave it some thought. "He will expect me there."

"Perhaps you will change at the party?" Jessamine's words were tight and her shoulders tense.

"Maybe one of your potions…" Zinnie suggested while she tapped her chin with one finger.

Jessamine dropped the cup she had been drying. It shattered to pieces on the floor. "Absolutely not!" she shouted at Zinnie.

Zinnie flinched at her response.

Jessamine composed herself. "Those potions are far too valuable to waste on a project like this one. A cloak and a wig shall serve you well in this situation." She turned away from Zinnie after picking up the remains of the broken mug.

Zinnie knew better than to argue. "Yes, Mistress."

She hesitantly approached Jessamine with her own mug and bowl and slid them onto the counter. "Is there anything else today?"

"No. Go." Jessamine waved her away.

Zinnie could have sworn she heard the woman's teeth grinding but decided not to stick around to find out what that had been all about.

"Lela, if I spend any more time with him, I will certainly change my mind. I must find a way to send him a message… Oh! I know!"

She scribbled a note on a parchment and tied it with one of her favorite lavender ribbons.

"Take this to him?" She handed it to Lela.

The dragon gave her a curious look.

"I've told him I have out of town relatives visiting and that I will not be able to see him for the next few days. I promised him I'd see him at the celebration at the end of the week, though. That should keep me from becoming too distracted while I make my final preparations."

Lela clicked her teeth and let out a puff of steam.

Zinnie rolled her eyes. "Trust me. It's for the best."

Although the prick in her heart argued otherwise.

She had to keep her resolve though if she was to pull this off for Jessamine.

She didn't expect the return note from Atlas with his sweet wishes for a pleasant visit and his strong desire to see her again.

"I'll be counting down the days until the celebration."

He had attached a single golden zinnia flower to his parchment.

When Lela dropped them in her lap, she gave Zinnie a knowing look.

Zinnie's heart leapt, and her lips pulled into a smile of their own accord. She sighed, and shoved the items into her satchel as she continued her errands.

She touched her lips where they had met his only hours before.

"You can do this, Zinnie. You can stay strong and not let your heart get carried away by his… all around perfectness."

Lela released a small flame at these words.

"Oh, hush. It must be done." Zinnie balled up her hand into a fist and lowered her eyebrows. "Come on, we have quite a to-do list to accomplish over the next three days."

The wigmaker would be the perfect place to find the first part of her disguise.

The bell over the door rang as she entered. The proprietor was someone she had "worked" with once or twice before, and he knew about discretion for his customers. Some women who had thinning hair and wished to disguise it, some men for the same reason, and others, like Zinnie, with less than honest reasons for needing a wig.

"What can I find for you today, young lady?" the man asked in a hushed tone.

Zinnie's eyes darted around the shop. No other

customers were present. That was a relief. She couldn't risk anyone finding out she had purchased a wig.

"Something subtle that will help me blend in to my surroundings. My… dim surroundings." Zinnie gave him a significant look.

"Ah, I see. How about one of these selections? Their lackluster shine and mousy color are perfect for staying… incognito."

Zinnie ran her hands over the wigs. The price tags showed they were out of her league. "Do you have anything more affordable? Perhaps one I could return after my needs have been met?"

The man's eyes twinkled. "It's not fancy, but it will do the trick if your… requirements… aren't too demanding?"

She nodded.

He went to the back of his shop and returned with a small box. Inside was a wig made from course hair, definitely not donated human hair, maybe that from a horse or something. It was long and stringy. She could imagine a scarf tied around her head like a cleaning woman, and the cloak covering that. She would never be recognized.

"It's perfect."

"And how would you like to pay for your borrowing of the item?" The man simpered a little with his question, ducking his head and raising his shoulders to his ears.

She gave him a sharp look. "I will keep my mistress from finding out about the…" she started to say.

He waved his hands in the air between their faces. "Yes, yes. No need to say anything further. Bring the item back in the condition in which it is now, and we shall call ourselves even."

Zinnie smiled at him and placed a hand on his shoulder. "Thank you, Millner."

He nodded and handed over the wig disguised in a simple circular hat box with a black ribbon looped at the top for a handle.

"I'll be back in two days to return it."

He gave her a kind wave as she exited the shop.

"Alright, Lela. This covers the disguise." She spoke to her friend who returned to the air as soon as they left the shop. "The dark cloak I already own should do the trick. My ankle boots should work well. Who knows if there'll be dancing like last time. And I'll need to be able to sneak around. We'll have to make sure my dress covers them, though, so that no one can get too good of a look at them."

Lela swooped low and pinched Zinnie's ear with her claws.

"Yes, Lela, so *Atlas* won't get a good look at them." She rolled her eyes. She ticked more items off her fingers. "The small satchel under the bed should be large enough to place the folded-up map inside. We'll need to make sure the dress has enough folds to hide the satchel beneath, too. Something with a long, full skirt should do the trick."

Lela made another cooing sound.

Zinnie gasped. "You're right. We'll need something to distract the badgerdragon as well. Got any suggestions?"

Chapter 31

Lela took to the air beside Zinnie and flew a few paces in front of her. She led Zinnie down the cobblestone streets, around the corner, and toward the aquarist. She hovered in front of a bucket filled with aquatic soft-shelled honeycrabs.

"You're a genius, Lela! This will be perfect. These will keep the creature busy for more than enough time for me to sneak in, grab the map, and sneak back to the party again."

Lela primped her feathers and batted her long lashes at the praise she received from Zinnie.

Zinnie giggled at her antics.

After they emerged from the aquarist, Zinnie held up one last finger.

She blew a curl off her eyelashes and sighed. "Now, for the dress."

Shopping for a new party dress would make any girl squeal with delight, swoon at the knees, and pull out their lacy fan to cool their excitement.

Normally, Zinnie would feel that way too, she was sure. But she never shopped for a dress for the right reasons. Only ever to pull a con. And this time, her mark was the man she had grown to love. It left a weight in the bottom of her stomach and a knot in her chest.

She squeezed her eyes shut, reminded herself that it had to be done, and forced her feet to carry her to her favorite costume shop used by the theater. They were always willing to lend her the clothing she needed because she always returned it in good condition and in a timely manner. The clothing sat in the back of a warehouse, totally unused most of the time.

The woman who kept the shop clean and dust free happily provided Zinnie with what she needed for the party.

"You're sure you don't mind?" Zinnie offered to pay in coins or trinkets from her purse.

"I insist. If anything, it brings me joy to see these clothes being worn so well by a pretty thing like you."

Zinnie grinned at the woman. "Thank you!"

With the midnight blue dress laid out on Zinnie's bed, her shoes settled neatly beside them, and the satchel stretched across the front, Zinnie could imagine how stunning she would look. The deep hue of the dress would enhance her features and blonde hair.

Atlas wouldn't be able to take his eyes off her. She didn't know if that was a good thing or not. He would certainly notice her missing.

But the feminine side of her wanted to look beautiful to him. She would find an excuse to leave his side long enough to steal the map and return before too much time passed.

The wig, wrapped in the cloak, rested in a bundle beside the dress. She would have to stash it outside the house or in the shadows of the entryway upon her arrival. That would be easy to do. A simple distraction would allow her to hide the bundle without anyone noticing.

She ran through the plan out loud, with Lela perched on top of the mirror, watching her with a keen eye.

"Hide the bundle. Mingle with the guests."

Lela huffed.

"Yes, Lela, I *know* I mean *Atlas*. I'm trying to *not* think about him all the time, remember? It's easier to say 'guests' instead of 'Atlas', alright?"

The dragon flapped her wings and settled herself on her perch again.

"*Anyway!*" Zinnie continued her plan. "Excuse myself to freshen up. Retrieve the bundle. Trick the badgerdragon. Steal the map. Discard the wig and cloak. Return to the party. That's it. Done and done."

Lela puffed out dark smoke.

"I know, and then I need to give the map to Jessamine. I get it."

But she didn't want to think about that part. She could pretend everything else was innocent. But once she left the party and gave the map to Jessamine, she would well and truly have stolen from Atlas. She will have betrayed him, once and for all. Then it would all come crashing down.

"That's why we'll *leave* after we bring the map back here," she said to Lela, as if the rest of her thoughts had been spoken out loud and not silently in her head.

"Speaking of which…" She bent down and dragged the case out from under her bed. She flipped back the lid and sat back on her heels to admire the long lengths of hair twined together and carefully stacked in a spiral inside the case.

"Do you think it will be long enough?"

Lela landed on the open lid and paced back and forth across it.

Zinnie sighed. "It will be, I know. It's just… maybe if I

found a *different* way for all of this to play out, I wouldn't have to leave. Wouldn't have to steal."

Lela sighed, too, though hers filled the air with a light mist.

Zinnie ran her hands along the braids and thought out loud of the potential alternatives. "Maybe we can steal a different map. Jessamine might not notice, right?"

Lela shot sparks out of her mouth.

"Careful, Lela! We don't want to catch the hair on fire, then where would we be?"

She shooed Lela off the case and secured the lid in place again. She plopped herself onto the floor with her elbows on her knees and her chin in her hands.

Her head bobbed up and down as she spoke with her bottom jaw stationary against her palms. "We could draw a fake map. Maybe I could even get Atlas to help me?"

Lela landed on one of her knees and gave her a sympathetic look.

Zinnie's volume dropped. "Maybe I could convince Atlas to run away with me. Leave all of this behind." Her breath caught.

He would never leave his family. And Jessamine would still not have the map. And then Lucy, Beatrice, and Felix would still be in danger.

Atlas said it himself. He would never allow his family to be harmed because of him ever again.

Only, this time, if harm befell them, it would be because of Zinnie.

A sob broke through her tight throat. There wasn't an alternative that would work. Stealing the map was the only way.

She lay on her side on the floor, resting her head on one outstretched arm and covering her face with the other. She allowed the tears to flow down her cheeks and onto the hard floor.

She deserved the discomfort that would await her if she fell asleep on the floor. She deserved *all* the discomfort and pain in the *world* for what she was supposed to do in just a few days.

A sharp whisper from Jessamine's shop awoke her sometime during the night.

The candle in her room had long since burned out. Lela remained curled in on herself in her unlocked cage, sleeping soundly.

Zinnie's back and hip ached from pressing onto the floor. Her hand was numb from her head resting on her arm.

The voices were muffled by the doors between herself and their source.

She groaned as quietly as possible as she sat up and scooted toward the door. She carefully pulled it open, not rising from the floor. She leaned against the door and focused her hearing on the sounds from right across the hall.

The phrases that Zinnie overheard sent chills down her spine.

"The full moon approaches. The experiment must succeed this time." Jessamine's voice sounded hushed but harsh.

"The creature has become dangerous. Kills indiscriminately. Monster." She only caught bits and pieces of the whispered male voice.

"This will be the perfect opportunity for a test," Jessamine demanded.

"Are you fully prepared for the consequences?" the man asked.

Jessamine's voice, louder than she probably intended, stabbed the quiet. "That is *none* of your concern. Just do it. *Now!*"

"Yes, Ma'am." The male voice turned submissive.

The back door closed.

Jessamine's impatient footsteps approached.

Zinnie quietly shut the door again, scurried to her bed, and flopped on top of the dress and shoes and satchel, face down on her pillow.

A cold sweat broke out on her neck and back.

If Jessamine knew she had overheard the conversation...

Chapter 32

The footsteps passed her door.

Jessamine's own door lock clicked.

Zinnie let out a sigh of relief.

"Did you hear that, Lela?" Zinnie whispered to her friend who had flown to her side as soon as the danger had passed. "What were they talking about? And do you think it has anything to do with… the map?"

Dread ate away at her so that she slept terribly the rest of the night. Fear racked her head and heart for Atlas and his family.

But also, a little for herself, too. Jessamine was a dangerous woman. If Zinnie didn't pull this off and make her escape, would she be the victim of the… *monster*… that the man had asked Jessamine about?

No matter what happened, she had to get the map to Jessamine, and leave the City of Dorian, before the full moon.

Before the sun rose, she measured the length of the braid in her case with a measuring ribbon. It gave her a good idea of how long the rope would be the night of her escape.

With a few more night's worth of hair added to it, she should have enough length to drop below the city and not die a horrible death on the rocks and debris below.

"Maybe I deserve a terrible death…" she murmured to herself as she made her way through the city towards the hole in the ground.

She peered through the hole. Told herself it, all of this, was for the best. Had Lela confirm the length one more time.

She sat there, staring. The temptation to run back, grab the braid, return right now, lower herself, and leave without another word to anyone was stronger than ever before.

But she promised herself she would do this one thing: steal the map; in order to protect Atlas's family.

As soon as she was finished, she would be gone before the sun rose on the city again.

Zinnie's reflection, even in the dingy mirror in her room, left her breathless. She thought she had looked so grown up the last time she dressed for a party, with her figure-accentuating dress and neatly-styled hair.

But this dress with its slightly wider neckline and figure accentuating bodice, her longer hair cascading over her shoulders in wavy curls, and the color in her cheeks and excitement in her eyes, would certainly stun Atlas as much as it did herself.

Lela took her place beneath Zinnie's hair, though she wouldn't have to stay there the whole time. She'd be able to show herself if she wanted to.

Zinnie stashed the satchel beneath the folds of her dress and patted the bundle on her bed.

The braid-rope sat securely beneath her bed. Her dark pants and blouse rested on top, ready for Zinnie to retrieve them when she returned home with the map.

Home.

The word caught in her mind. Would she miss this place? The only home she could remember?

She turned in a slow circle. The cracked, warped mirror had been her only friend for so many years before she had found Lela. But she would find a clear one wherever she ended up.

She fingered her comb and tucked it inside the case with her hair. It wasn't anything special, but it had been the source of comfort in her loneliness as she combed her hair and cut it every day.

That reminded her. She reached beneath her bodice and pulled out her lock-picking tools. She touched each one to make sure they were all there. Her fingers lingered on the dull, rusty scissors. The first thing she would obtain for herself after she found her way somewhere new would be a nice, shiny pair of scissors, so sharp that they would slice through her thick locks with ease.

The imagery made her smile.

This path that she was being forced to take tonight may not be perfect, but it *would* be hers. She would *own it*. Do her job *perfectly*. And leave on her own terms once and for all.

She lifted her chin, replaced the tools beneath her bodice, grabbed the bundle and headed for the door. She took one last look over her shoulder before she exited.

"Here goes nothing," she said under her breath.

The Forster mansion was as familiar as it had been all the other times she had been there, not like the first time when she had felt like an intruder at the party. This time all four family members welcomed her with open arms.

"How was your visit with your relatives?" Beatrice asked as she stroked Lela's iridescent feathers.

Zinnie, prepared as always for all the possible questions she may encounter, had a response ready.

"Aunt Zelda and Uncle Henry came. They brought along their sweet little children, Margaret and Michael. I had so much fun playing games with them while the adults caught up. I hope to see them again before too long." The lies came as easy as truths would have.

The others spent a few minutes playing with Lela before the dragon took up her hiding place again. Even though the Forster's didn't mind Lela's presence, others at the party may not be so accepting.

Atlas remained close by her side and escorted her around the room as he greeted his parents' guests.

Zinnie avoided eye contact with those who may recognize her, but she knew no one would say anything. Everyone had too much at stake with Jessamine to risk offending or exposing Zinnie's true identity. She did notice a few raised eyebrows and whispers behind hands.

At least Jessamine would hear that Zinnie played her part well.

There was no dancing at the party this time. The family must have received word that such a thing at a soiree was frowned upon. A dance must be advertised as such, and a soiree was only food and visiting.

Zinnie was a little relieved. She didn't know if she would go through with her plan if she had to be so close to Atlas during a dance. As it was, she had a hard time focusing on anything except his perfect lips and shining eyes filled with joy. She was sure her own face reflected the same thing.

Zinnie waited for just the right moment to slip away and perform her task, but the moment just wouldn't present itself. She didn't want to tear herself from Atlas's side. She didn't want to feel the absence of his hand on her back, or her hand resting in the crook of his arm. She didn't want to miss a single whispered comment in her ear that left tingles running down her neck.

Just like the last time, Atlas eventually led her outside into the garden for fresh air. He slipped his hand down her arm and laced his fingers between her own.

They strolled around the tidy garden together, making small talk about the other guests, reminiscing about the midsummer lights and the incredible display of glowing creatures that had surrounded them that night.

Atlas led Zinnie to the spot where they had picnicked before. A blanket spread across the ground. Two small plates of her favorite sweet pastries rested right in the middle. The clear sky and bright almost-full moon gave just the right amount of light for a romantic ambiance.

"Join me?" Atlas helped Zinnie lower herself to the ground and arrange her full skirts around her. She sat on one hip, with her legs and feet curled to one side.

While Zinnie shifted her skirts around her legs and feet, Lela soared skyward to hunt for a snack. Zinnie didn't mind the privacy she would have with Atlas that Lela's absence would provide.

Atlas joined her on the other side, so she could lean against him instead of supporting herself with one of her own arms propped against the ground.

She relaxed and leaned her head against his shoulder. He stroked her long curls and caressed her hand in his lap.

"It feels so good to have you with me again. I've missed you these past few days," Atlas murmured quietly to her.

Zinnie nodded. "Me, too."

"I hope I never have to go that many days without seeing you again." He kissed the top of her head.

She shivered from the contact. And from the guilt that plagued her.

Before she could even think of a response, he pulled a parcel from his jacket pocket. "I have a gift for you."

She sat up differently so she could face him and take the small, velvet box from his hands.

She gasped and darted her glance from the box to his eyes and back again. "Oh, Atlas!"

Had he purchased jewelry for her? She wasn't deserving of an expensive gift that would come in a box like this.

"I shouldn't." She pushed the box toward his hand again. She shook her head and willed herself not to start crying.

"Did you know your eyes are even more beautiful when you cry? They sparkle. Although, I promise that wasn't my intent tonight!" His smile was warm and sincere.

He took the box from her and opened it toward himself. He turned the open container so she could see the contents.

This time the tears would not stay inside. She stared at the most beautiful pair of scissors she had ever seen.

Chapter 33

"How did you know?" She touched the scissors with a timid finger before lifting them from the box.

The handles had several swirls of metal like her own curls that landed in her lap every time she cut her hair. The sharp blades sparkled in the moonlight.

He laughed in a loving way and his grin stretched from ear to ear. "I thought that if you have to cut that beautiful, thick hair every day in order to keep yourself from tripping on the curls, you deserved the perfect scissors. I found this from a metalsmith that imbues his works with dwarf magic."

Zinnie knew exactly who he talked about. The dwarf metalsmith in town named Ironforge. She had done business with him herself but did not mention that to Atlas.

"He promised they would never dull. Do you like them?"

She let out a soft, incredulous laugh. "I love them! But really? He just *happened* to have a pair of magically sharp scissors like this lying around?" Her eyes left the scissors and landed on Atlas's face again.

He touched the side of her face. "I designed them myself and commissioned him to make them for me. For you."

He leaned closer and looked at her lips.

She held still and allowed him to close the gap until their lips met.

The pure love that embraced her entire body like a warm hug led her to wrap her arms around his neck. He pulled her a little closer, and they shared a deeper kiss.

"Zinnie, *I love you*," he said when he finally pulled away just far enough to say the words but close enough that she felt them on her face.

Her eyes filled with tears that spilled down her cheeks. "I love you, Atlas."

Her heart finally shattered, just like she feared.

He furrowed his brow. "You don't look happy, Zinnie…"

She shook her head. She couldn't find her voice between the sobs that threatened to overtake her body. She barely held them in with steady deep breaths.

"I am happy with you, Atlas. This, *you*, are a dream come true for me. Something I never thought I would have. Something I certainly don't deserve."

The tears flowed; the sobs shook her shoulders. She brought her knees up to her face and buried her head in them. She couldn't bear to face him now.

His strong arms wrapped around her shoulders as he scooted closer and pulled her against his chest. He stroked her hair. "Whatever the problem is, I will help you. I will do anything I can to solve your troubled heart. *Anything*."

She knew the words were true. This was Atlas. He bore the burdens of everyone around him. He would bear hers, too. All she had to do was ask.

If only that were possible.

He soothed her with his calm voice, rubbed her back, and kissed her hair and forehead while he waited for her to speak.

To somehow explain whatever this trauma was that weighed her down so much that she couldn't even enjoy a romantic moment with the love of her life.

Eventually, after much too long for Zinnie's liking, her tears slowed, and her breathing returned to normal. She leaned away from him so she could see his face.

What was she going to do? *She loved him.* With everything that she had. She couldn't keep secrets from him anymore, even if it meant he rejected her once and for all.

She *promised* herself she would protect him, and she would, but that didn't mean she couldn't at least tell him the truth first.

"I don't know how to tell you," she whispered and searched his eyes.

He looked confused and stroked her arms with both hands. "You can trust me with anything."

She nodded. Wiped a few more tears from her cheeks, and prepared herself to confess everything to him, at last.

She braced herself for his reaction and told herself that even if he hated her for it, at least she would be able to live her life knowing that she had kept nothing from him in the end.

The precious gift of magical scissors lay forgotten on the blanket beside them as she opened herself up to Atlas and told him everything, all the way from the beginning.

Everything about her parents stealing phoenix tears from Jessamine when Zinnie was a baby. How they had mysteriously died when she was a toddler. How Jessamine had taken her in and taught her everything she had learned. All the ladylike lessons, and all the sleight of hand, power of suggestion, art of deception, and how to steal, lie, and cheat her way out of any situation.

Atlas furrowed his brow. His mouth turned down in a frown. She avoided looking at him and finished.

Jessamine had hired out Zinnie's skills for the woman's own personal gain. Zinnie had been a rogue, a thief, and a liar for as long as she could remember.

Atlas sat in stunned silence when Zinnie finished talking.

She stared at her own hands, not daring to look at his face. She didn't think she'd be able to bear the look he might give her. Either pity, dismay, or rejection. It didn't matter. Any of those reactions would be too much.

Atlas muttered something, but Zinnie held her hand up to silence him.

"Wait, I'm not quite finished. There's a little bit more." The tears dripped down her face.

He did not reach up to tenderly wipe them away this time. His lack of affection stung, but she pressed on.

"My current job for Jessamine is…" She took a deep breath, held it for a second, and let it out. She would look him in the eye as she finished her confession. No matter the cost.

She made eye contact. "To steal something from your father."

She held her breath.

He opened his mouth, then snapped it closed again. A range of emotions flashed in his eyes and across his face.

"Before you say anything," she continued. "I need to tell you everything. I don't want to leave anything out. I posed as a cleaning girl when you first moved here to case your home.

"I broke in at night once to steal the item Jessamine wants, but your badgerdragon sounded the alarm that chased me away."

She swiped her tears from her cheeks with the palm of one hand.

"I am supposed to sneak away from the party, from you, tonight to steal from your father's study."

She held her chin high and straightened her shoulders.

"*You* were my mark all this time, Atlas. I was tasked to get close to you so I could have an in with your home, your family. If it wasn't for all of that, we never would have met or spent time together."

A memory flashed in her mind. She laughed at herself. "Actually, we did meet, before Jessamine told me to con your family. The day you arrived. I dropped my handkerchief, and you returned it to me. In that moment I knew you were different than everyone else in this dreadful place."

In that moment, she thought to herself, *you already had a piece of my heart.*

She didn't confess those feelings. It would seem forced. Fake. To further the con.

Atlas let out a long sigh. He ran his fingers through his hair and fidgeted with his hands.

Zinnie kept her hands folded tight in her own lap. She knew that any tender touches that may have happened that night would no longer take place. A chasm had opened between them. Their connection severed.

"What… how…" Atlas sighed again. "I honestly don't even know what to say."

She waited for him to process the news.

"Was any of it real?" he whispered.

Tears continued to flow from Zinnie's eyes, though the sobs had ended. "Yes, Atlas. I stole the medicine for your family from Jessamine. I watched over you while you were sick, begged the heavens to let you live."

She wanted so badly to feel his arms around her again, but it would be too much to ask.

When his hand covered hers in her lap, she nearly jumped out of her skin.

"Zinnie, I don't blame you for the life you've been forced to live. I can't imagine the pain you've been through and the burdens you've had to carry on your own. Please know that.

I care for you, Zinnie, but I don't know if the *you* I fell in love with is the real thing or not. I need some time to think."

"I understand." Zinnie shifted so she could stand.

Atlas did not release his grip of her hand. He tugged her toward the ground.

"I wish for you to stay…" His moist eyes looked hurt and confused.

She sat beside him in uncomfortable silence.

He was surely replaying every interaction they experienced over and over in his head and analyzing them from a different perspective.

She did the same. Would he see that she had meant it? That she really did love him?

He finally spoke again. "What was it you were meant to steal? From my father I mean?" His quiet voice was filled with pain and now he avoided eye contact with her.

"A specific map."

He nodded. "I believe I know the one…"

"I don't really even care about the map anymore, Atlas. I haven't for some time. But she has threatened your family. I don't know what she has planned but she commanded that I return with the map before the full moon."

She looked at the sky. It was only two days away. It really was now or never.

"She is capable of much evil. If I don't steal the map, I don't think your family will live." Her voice cracked. "That's why I came tonight and planned to go through with it. But there has to be another way. I will take the punishment. Beg her until my last breath."

"I could never let you…" Atlas began.

"No. You are a good person. Your whole family are good people. Better than I knew existed. I have never felt so loved as I have in your home, even before I developed feelings for you. You deserve so much better than a villain like me. I will make up some story about how you don't have the map after all. It was destroyed in transport, or someone else already stole it. Then she will have no reason to unleash her worst on your family."

"No. If she is as you say, that would end poorly for you. I can't let you do that for us. For me. Everything you told me does change things, but you still have my heart."

Zinnie cried again and covered her face with her hands. "I don't deserve to be loved by someone like you. I can endure whatever she has in store, but your family will be safe. It's the only way."

Atlas stood and pulled her to stand beside him. He held her hand and stepped toward the outer walls of the garden.

"Where are we going, Atlas?"

Was he turning her in? Was she going to be in trouble with his parents? With the guards?

Chapter 34

e're going to my father's study to get the map she wants. If she wants it that badly, she can have it."

Zinnie yanked her hand from his and skidded to a stop. "No, Atlas. She shouldn't have it. No good can come from her obtaining something that she wants this much."

"But it will keep you safe. I don't care about some piece of paper. You can stay here, stay away from her. You are good, Zinnie, no matter what you have been led to believe."

"How can you say that? I've told you only a fraction of the things I've done for her. If you knew, you wouldn't say that."

He stepped close and took her hands. "I am hurt by your deception. I need time to heal before I can move on with whatever is growing between us. But I am not ready to let you go, either."

"You must, Atlas. It's the only way. I'm sorry. And I do love you more than I thought I would ever love anyone."

She ran from the garden, through the house and out the front door. She left her cloak and wig behind. Tears blurred her vision. She headed straight for Jessamine's shop, not worried in the slightest about Lela catching up to her, or who might have seen her or followed her or anything.

She pushed through the back door and slunk her way to her room. She couldn't face Jessamine now. It wouldn't matter if she admitted her failure now or in the morning. The punishment would be swift and harsh. For herself *and* for the Forster's, she was afraid.

The best she could do was formulate a believable story and attempt to buy more time to accomplish the task.

Just as the midnight evening gown slipped from her shoulders and landed in a heap on the floor, Jessamine entered the room without a knock. She closed the door with a snap and stood only two paces from Zinnie, her arms folded across her chest.

Lela slipped through the door before Jessamine closed it. Zinnie felt instant comfort by the dragon's presence.

"I trust you have returned with your quarry?" Jessamine extended her hand to Zinnie for the map.

Zinnie kicked away the dress and folded her arms around herself. Her thin sleeping dress that had doubled as her underlayer beneath the finer dress left her chilled. She rubbed the goosebumps on her arms to try to warm up. She also wracked her brain for the most believable story she could muster. She willed herself to speak calmly and not give anything away.

She composed herself in an instant and shook her head. She put a glum expression on her face. "I'm sorry, Mistress. Atlas's father's last shipment of belongings was robbed on the way to Dorian. All their belongings have been stolen, including the map in question."

Jessamine raised one eyebrow. "Your deceitfulness has improved, Little Flower."

Zinnie winced but tried to cover it up with a yawn. "I'm sure we'll figure something out tomorrow."

Jessamine reached behind her and opened the door. Her raven from the shop swooped in and landed on the top of Zinnie's mirror.

Lela's feather fluffed at the arrival of the raven. She cowered at the back of Zinnie's neck.

"A little birdie has told me quite a different story. You told Atlas everything. The boy even *offered* you the map, yet you *refused to take it*. I can't believe you would betray me like this, Zinnie."

Zinnie flinched. She couldn't remember the last time Jessamine had used her given name. Almost as if using it humanized Zinnie too much. It was easier to think of her as a tool if she gave her a meaningless nickname. But now that Zinnie had betrayed her, the woman saw her as an adversary instead of an asset.

Jessamine took a step closer to Zinnie. She clicked her tongue and shook her head. She tapped Zinnie on the head with one of her falsely youthful hands. "What are we going to do with you?"

Zinnie stared at Jessamine with wide eyes.

"Manticore got your tongue, little one?" Jessamine leaned close to Zinnie's face.

All the blood left Zinnie's face. Her head spun. Her hands shook.

"I see through your mask. I know your secrets. You love him. You love his family even though they have done *nothing* for you, and I have done *everything* for you for *years*." Jessamine's voice rose in volume. She punctuated her words with flicks of her hand near Zinnie's face.

Zinnie flinched but held still. She didn't shrink from her

mistress. Jessamine did not like shows of weakness. It would be better for Zinnie to stand her ground, but not to argue or disagree in the slightest.

And her mistress might be aware of most of Zinnie's secrets, but there was one she still had no idea about. The case full of Zinnie's hair, braided into a rope strong enough and long enough for Zinnie to leave the city, and Jessamine's control.

As soon as the woman left, Zinnie would pack her few belongings and be gone. Then Jessamine couldn't threaten her anymore.

Her heart stung at the memory of the forgotten scissors from Atlas on the blanket in the garden. She would have treasured them for her lifetime if she had remembered to bring them with her. But she was wholly undeserving of any form of gift or kindness like that. It was for the best.

She refocused her mind on the present. Jessamine continued to lecture her at full volume about Zinnie's failures.

"But it doesn't matter what you do now." Her voice grew eerily calm. She looked down her nose at Zinnie. "I will send my wolf hybrid to retrieve the map. Or, at least, to clear the path for me so I may retrieve it myself."

Zinnie's eyes widened. "No, Jessamine. You can't! Please!"

Jessamine's nostrils flared at the sound of her name from Zinnie's lips.

Zinnie ignored her. "I'll do anything." Here she was, begging just like Atlas had insisted she shouldn't.

"You will return to the house. You will retrieve the map I want by any means necessary. You will return it to me. Then we shall discuss your punishment for your lies and defiance. I have allowed you entirely too much freedom. If you do not pull this off by the end of the day tomorrow, you will regret ever having shown up on my doorstep. And the Forster's will regret having come to the City of Dorian at all."

Zinnie nodded. Her eyes had no tears left in them after the evening she had spent crying in Atlas's garden. "Yes, ma'am."

All hopes of fleeing the city vanished. She would sacrifice her freedom to protect the Forster's. Perhaps this one good act would somehow redeem herself for all the terrible things she had done her entire life. It's all she could hope for.

There would be no chance to escape once she gave the map to Jessamine. The woman would make sure of it. She would remain trapped in this city forever. She might as well be trapped in the tower from her dreams with no stairs, no door, no way of escape.

Jessamine patted her head again. "Good girl. Now get some sleep. Your eyes are puffy, and your hair is a mess." She flicked Zinnie's long locks with her finger, turned, and marched from the room. She held the door open a moment too long to allow the raven to follow her.

Zinnie donned her regular green work dress, cut the last lock of curls from last night's party and added them to her box, and collected Lela to go to Atlas's house.

How would she get the map? Would she just knock on the door and ask for it? Would she sneak in and steal it when no one was paying attention? Would Atlas be there? Would he want to see her?

Her eyes stung and her stomach ached from the waves of emotions that crashed over her. How had her life come to this? She knew better than to become attached to a mark. It was one of the first rules of the con. And it always, *always* ended poorly. No matter what.

But she had walked right into it and now here she was trying to clean up the mess without hurting anyone else.

She nearly tripped on the bundle that rested right outside

the back door to the shop. It was her cloak. The wig rested in a heap on top. She had forgotten that she needed to return the wig. *And* the dress, now that she thought about it.

Her heart sank. More evidence that she was a liar who didn't deserve Atlas's love.

Beneath the wig she discovered a thick envelope with a fresh wax seal on it. She picked it up, looked both ways down the alley, but saw no one.

Maybe her lessons in stealth had taken hold with Atlas after all. A smirk pulled on her lips. *Well done, Atlas.*

She scooped up the bundle and carried it back to her room. She smoothed the dress on her bed to try to remove some of the wrinkles before she would return it later. She settled on the stool in front of the mirror to see what the envelope contained.

She pulled out a torn piece of parchment with a hastily scrawled note on it. "I can't lose you forever, Zinnie. Give the map to Jessamine. Come to my home, where you'll be safe. Please." He signed it with only a capital "*A.*"

Her heart leaped. She pulled out the map. It was the very one that Jessamine had described.

He had given it to her. Had given it up for *her.*

He deserved so much better.

And even though he said she would be safe, as long as she stayed in the city, she would never truly be safe from Jessamine's control. Too many people knew her. Knew of her connections with the woman. She would never be able to hide once Jessamine put out the word that she had run away.

"This is it, Lela. We can protect Atlas. Give Jessamine what she wants- even though the consequences are sure to be disastrous for someone, sometime- and execute our escape plan. Everyone will be safe. Everyone wins."

Lela breathed a steady stream of fire toward Zinnie.

Zinnie yanked the map away before it caught on fire.

"Lela! What has come over you!"

The dragon growled a deep grumble inside her chest. The sound was not intimidating, because she was so small, but the meaning was clear.

"I *have* to do this, Lela. It is for the best. For everyone."

Chapter 35

Everything went as smoothly as she planned. She left the map for Jessamine on her pillow. The woman would be furious that Zinnie had broken into her room. She believed her lock to be impenetrable. But she would have what she wanted.

Zinnie packed her few belongings in her satchel and slung it across her shoulder, donned her dark pants and blouse, covered herself in her cloak, and lugged the case through the city. Lela hovered beside her the entire way.

Her movements were agitated, just like Zinnie's emotions.

She placed the case in a hiding spot.

"Just one stop first, Lela, and then we'll leave."

She made her way through the shadows to Atlas's house before the sun came up.

"Wait here," she said to Lela.

She climbed the outside wall.

Slipped through his window.

She watched him sleep for several blessed seconds. Soaked in all of him. Promised herself she would never forget him.

She left a note on the foot of his bed. It explained that she had given the map to Jessamine, fled the city, and would never return. She expressed her love for him and her gratitude for everything he had taught her about family and love. She bid him goodbye. Forever.

The full moon hung low in the sky when she lowered the long, braided rope through the hole and secured it to the hitching post outside the feathercorn stable so that it would hold. She peered through the gap to the beach below.

"Am I really doing this, Lela? He was too good to be true, wasn't he? And if I stay, Jessamine will *never* let me go. I will never get to be with Atlas either way. At least this way, I will be free."

By the time she slid down the entire length of rope to the rocks below, Lela by her side the entire way, her leather gloves were smooth from the friction. She hesitated at the bottom. She had done it. She had left the city. Her plan had worked.

She gazed up the rope to the tiny hole high above her head. "The City of Dorian will be nothing but a distant memory from now on."

She reached one of her booted feet toward the sand beneath her. She stepped down slowly. Gingerly placed her foot on the ground, half expecting to be held back by the same invisible barrier that had prevented her from leaving the city her entire life. But her foot connected. She let go of the rope made from her own locks of hair.

She had done it. She had cracked one final lock, and she had obtained her freedom.

When she released the hair rope, Lela released a stream of

white-hot fire that ignited the braided rope. The hair singed and smoked as the fire spread all the way to the very top. All evidence of Zinnie's escape disappeared in the flames.

Zinnie collapsed on the sand, removed her gloves, and let the softness run through her fingers.

She jumped to her feet and screamed in elation at her newfound freedom.

She dropped to her knees and cried tears of loss for the years that had been stolen from her, and the future she could have had with Atlas if only everything had been different.

But it didn't matter. It was all in her past.

This was the first day of her new life.

"Come on, Lela. Let's see what Tala has to offer!"

She wiped the tears from her cheeks. Stood on her feet. Walked away from the braided rope. And didn't look back.

It had only been a few hours since she left the city, and already her senses had been overwhelmed by all the newness of the world around her. Wonder filled her heart at everything that had been kept from her all these years.

She didn't make very quick progress. Between herself and Lela stopping so often to examine a flower that had fangs or a creature that looked like a stick but moved like a grasshopper, they traveled at a snail's pace.

She followed the road that led away from Dorian toward the Graufast Mountains. The very road that Atlas had traveled to move to the City of Dorian.

"Zinnie! Wait!" A familiar voice called from behind.

Lela flipped in the air and ruffled her feathers. Zinnie followed her with her eyes until she spotted the source of the voice.

"Atlas?" The name passed her lips in barely above a whisper. "How can it be?"

She stood still and waited for the apparition to either fade or solidify. She had heard of creatures that could make you see things that weren't really there, and herbs that could alter your sense of reality. Had she come into contact with one or the other? Was her mind playing tricks on her?

He ran toward her on his own two feet and skidded to a stop only an arm's length away.

He doubled over and rested his hands on his knees to catch his breath.

"Atlas?" She asked him to his face this time.

He held out one finger to indicate for her to wait while he caught his breath.

"Do you... do you need a drink?" She offered her canteen.

"Thank you," he wheezed. He gulped from the bottle, wiped his face with the back of his hand, and returned the canteen to Zinnie.

"What are you doing here?" she asked him.

She looked past him to see if he had come alone.

Just at the edge of her vision she saw a wagon pulled by a pair of feathered oxen. "Is that your family? I'm so confused. What's going on?"

"You forgot something." He reached into his pocket and removed the same velvety box that he had presented to her in his garden. "I couldn't let you leave without your gift. How else are you to maintain that fast-growing hair of yours?" He gave her a mischievous grin.

When she didn't reach for the box, he pulled her hand toward him and set the box into it.

She opened it with her other hand and there were the beautiful scissors that he had given to her.

She sucked in a sharp breath and her eyes darted back to his.

"I... I don't understand..."

"Zinnie, you challenged my perception of good verses bad in a way I never imagined. You made me see the world through different eyes. Helped me figure out who I am and who I want to become. Your passion for life inspires me. You do whatever you want and have no fear."

She shrunk from his enthusiasm. "But what about all the bad things I've done?"

He shook his head. "What about all the *good* things you've done?"

She looked at the ground. "I haven't done much good."

He stepped closer and took her hands. Only kindness radiated from his face. "I see the good in you that you have been trained to not see. The only reason you learned to do the things you did was because you were forced to. It was the only way to survive. But you used your skills in positive ways too. You were kind to those less fortunate than you. You protected others from Jessamine as often as you could. You gave of yourself even when you were forced to take from others. You sought a way out of this life for a long time."

"But…"

"You saved your hair for how long in order to escape? No one would even think to do that if they were satisfied with the life that they had to live. Why did you do it, Zinnie? *Why* did you leave?"

His question was not filled with hurt. He was sincerely asking her.

She thought for a long moment. "To find a better life." She shrugged and looked away.

"Exactly."

She slipped her hands from his and turned away. "Those are all excuses bad people tell themselves to ease their conscience from the truth. I am not a good person, Atlas."

He gently turned her face toward him again with his hand. "These are not excuses, Zinnie. They are the truth."

"Zinnie!" Lucy jumped from the wagon and ran toward Zinnie. She threw her arms around her in a warm embrace.

Zinnie gave Atlas a questioning look over his sister's shoulder.

"They know, Zinnie. And they agree with you. The City of Dorian is toxic."

"He's right," Beatrice chimed in when the wagon caught up with the teenagers. "We have left it behind us."

Felix nodded beside his wife. "No matter how rich or important those people could make us feel, we would be fools to stay there a moment longer than necessary. You showed us this, Zinnie. Thank you for saving my family from a lifetime of disappointment. Or worse."

Lela flew circles around the family, singing in her cooing way her joy at seeing them again.

Zinnie couldn't believe this. "You are all mistaken about me. I don't know what Atlas told you, but…"

Beatrice disembarked from the wagon and strolled toward Zinnie. She wrapped her arms around Zinnie in the sweetest motherly way that Zinnie had always dreamed of but never experienced.

Tears streamed down Zinnie's face. Her knees nearly gave out.

This, right here, *this* is always what she had wanted.

"You deserve *everything*, Zinnie. And we are here to make sure you find it all," Beatrice whispered in her ear.

"Now," Felix interrupted, "I believe Atlas has something else he would like to say."

"I do, thank you, Father."

Beatrice stepped away and Atlas replaced her in front of Zinnie.

"Zinnie, I love you. I would love to get to know the *real* you, however much of it I don't already know. Will you please join our family as we travel Tala to find a new home?"

Zinnie couldn't believe this. They loved her? Even after everything she had done?

"I don't know what to say." For the first time in her life,

she was at a total loss for words, truthful or deceitful.

Atlas pulled her into his arms and kissed her sweetly on the lips. He whispered into her ear. "Say you'll come. Please?"

Lela landed on Zinnie's shoulder and blew smoke from her nostrils, as if she were threatening Zinnie to answer the right way… or else.

She nodded. "Yes, Atlas. I'll follow you to the ends of Tala if that's where you'll go."

"Actually," Atlas pulled away to look her in the eye. "I was kind of thinking of following *you* if you don't mind. Where do *you* want to go, Zinnie? We'll tag along for the journey."

Zinnie smiled. "Everywhere."

Thank you for Reading!

I hope you enjoyed this book!
Please leave a review on **Amazon** and **Goodreads**. For indie authors like me, reviews are our lifeblood. Help a girl out, it'll only take a few minutes!

Check me out on social media!

Facebook: Christine K. Marshall-author
www.facebook.com/christinemarshallauthor

Instagram: @the_christine_marshall_24
www.instagram.com/the_christine_marshall_24

TikTok: www.tiktok.com/@christinemarshallfantasy

Email: christinemarshall24@gmail.com

Welcome to Tala!

All of Christine's fantasy books take place in one fantasy world called **Tala**, pronounced "**tall**-uh."

Each series or standalone book can be read in any order in relation to the other series or books.

You'll see character crossovers, hidden secrets, and clues to the other stories, characters, and settings as you read the collection. The more you read, the deeper you'll understand Tala and all the characters that live there.

Here's a chronological diagram if you prefer reading in chronological order. Otherwise, pick a book or series that sounds good to you and start there!

Enjoy exploring Tala!

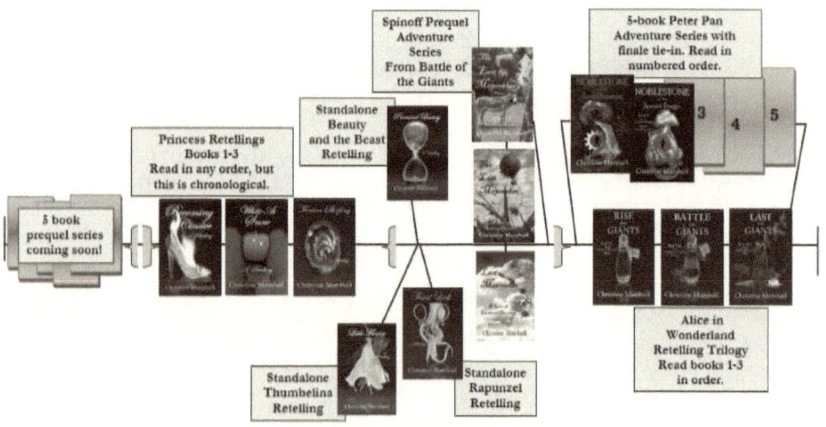

Keep turning pages to learn about each book in the collection (so far!) and don't forget to sign up for Christine's e-newsletter for all the latest news and updates for future books.

Find all Christine's books at CMarshallFantasy Etsy shop and Amazon today.

Buy direct!
CMarshallFantasy
Etsy

Order from
Amazon here

Here's why you'll love these books:

~Mythical creatures like centaurs, griffins, pixies, brownies, elves, golems, giants (of course!), and so many more.

~Magic that prolongs life and heals, and attracts the wrong kind of attention.

~People who can talk to animals and make flowers blossom just by touch.

~Stories of friendship, romance, family connections, and epic journeys that will keep you reading for hours.

Princess Retellings

When Cinderella becomes the villain of her story...
and all the other stories, too.
A villain origin story for the biggest villain in all of Tala.

What if Cinderella was already a princess?
What if her step-sisters weren't mean?
What if her family, her crown... and her love were ripped
away from her?
What if in her grief she made a terrible mistake?
Maybe not all fairy-tales end with happily ever after...

Read *Becoming Cinder* today!
Available in print, ebook, and audiobook.

What happens to Jessamine next?
Why does Juliette ask Jessamine to come home?
What happened to Peter?
Read the next book in the series from Juliette's perspective.

A princess in hiding.
A huntsman as her protector.
Seven unlikely companions by her side.
Can she stop the growing evil threatening her world?

Add *White As Snow* to your bookshelf now!

Available in print, ebook, and audiobook.

Your new favorite *Beauty and the Beast* retelling: ***Promised Beauty***

What if *Beauty* seeks out the Beast?
What if he wants her to *leave*, but she *refuses*?
What if neither of them are looking for *love*,
but find it in the most *unexpected* place?
A tale as old as time, told with a few new twists.

Add this new instant classic to your fairytale collection today!

Available in print and ebook.

The *Charlie and the Giants* trilogy
inspired by *Alice in Wonderland*.

Fifteen-year-old Charlie leaves home and ventures into the unknown to battle monsters, befriend fairies and giants, and discover who she really is. Oh, and try to save the world.

What happens when the land of wonder is broken upon Charlie's return?

Who will she find this time to help her put an end once and for all to the evil that has spread?

How can a girl full of dreams face the reality of what must be done?

A tale of strange creatures, twists and turns, and ever-growing darkness.

The final chapter in an epic saga of fairy tales, princesses, and a world of dreams.
From the Queen of Cinders to the Queen of All.
From a powerless princess to a Princess of power.
From a girl with dreams to a Dreamer destined to save the world.

Christine's ***Charlie and the Giants*** books are filled with magic, mythical creatures, and an *awesome* female protagonist that has to figure out who she wants to become.

If you love books that will help you forget the real world for a little while, are full of surprising characters, and will keep you guessing, then these are the perfect books for you!

Available in print, ebook, and audiobook.

Get ready for another exciting fantasy adventure!

Steampunk? *Check!*
Pirates? *Check!*
Dwarves? *Check!*
Peter Pan vibes? *Check!*

These books are perfect for readers young and old who love friendship, family, and adventure!

Amazon.com: Noblestone and the Lost Dwarves: 9798...
www.amazon.com

Noblestone and the Lost Dwarves Paperback - Etsy
www.etsy.com

The Last Mapmaker:
A Series of Intentional Disasters
A spinoff humor series

Readers young and old will fall in love with brownie
brothers Max and Eliot who have a penchant for mischief
as they go on a series of crazy adventures.
These guys will make you laugh and keep you turning
pages.

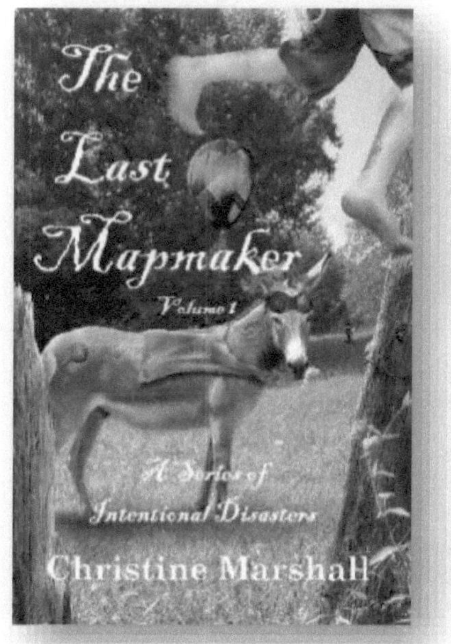

Available in print and ebook.

Join brownie brothers Max and Eliot as they go on
another wild adventure, this time into the clouds. Tag
along as they encounter cloud dragons, giants, mermaids,
and leave a trail of mayhem in their path.
You'll laugh til you cry and then laugh some more.

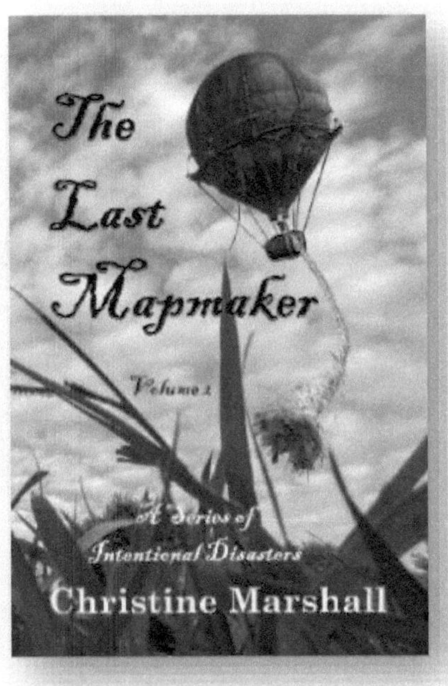

Available in print and ebook.

Fantasy world? Check!
Playful antics? Check!
Fun for the whole family? Check!
Positive sibling relationships? Check!

Let Max and Eliot take you on another exciting
adventure!

The Last Mapmaker Volume 3: A Series of
Intentional Disasters (Charlie and the Giants):
Marshall, Christine: 9781965310021:
Amazon.com: Books

www.amazon.com

CMarshallFantasy Etsy

Also see what kind of trouble these two cause in
the ***Charlie and the Giants*** series where they make their
appearance in ***Battle of the Giants.***

Available in print and ebook.

Read our Illustrated Guides of Tala!

Insects & Mechanical Things

Dragons & Flying Creatures

Unexpected Creatures

Folk Creatures

Order Here! 

Coming 2026

A *Little Mermaid* Retelling

Sign up for Christine's e-newsletter!

Check out Christine's website!

www.ChristineMarshallAuthor.com

Christine's Amazon author page:

E&O Creative's Etsy shop
Featuring art by Steve, signed books by Christine,
and other awesome swag!

Coloring books featuring illustrations from Steve including
chapter heading art from Christine's books!

Acknowledgements

Final Lock would not have been possible without a lot of amazing people!

Beta readers: Steve, Sophie, and Pepper. Y'all rock!

Original cover art & chapter heading art: my amazing husband, **Steve**, thank you for being my love story inspiration… again! 💕
And thank you for the collaboration on the story and the art. I love you too much.

ARC readers, promo team, friends, and other awesome supporters: Chantelle, Tanya, Cali, Sarah, Kate, Miranda, Jennie, Catie, Ashlee, Joanne, Sherri (& Taco!), Lianne, A. Perdue, Abbie, Samantha, Mike, Crina, and so many more- thank you for continuing to share my books and supporting us in our publishing journey! We are blessed to know you all!!

To everyone who has read, shared, and reviewed my books, thank you!

About the Author

When Christine isn't spinning tales on her laptop, she probably has a book and a chocolate chip cookie in hand. She loves all kinds of books: fantasy, sci-fi, historical fiction, non-fiction, and even textbooks.

She also loves to play her ukulele, stand in the rain, stay up late, and try new foods... but not all at the same time! Christine has moved over 20 times in the past 20 years, and firmly believes that people are more important than things.

Photo Credit: Amber Richards

www.ingramcontent.com/pod-product-compliance
Lightning Source LLC
Chambersburg PA
CBHW020128310726
48970CB00006B/1775